A WORLD FULL OF ANIMAL STORIES

WRITTEN BY ANGELA McALLISTER

ILLUSTRATED BY AITCH

Frances Lincoln
Children's Books

CONTENTS

EUROPE

AUSTRALIA AND OCEANIA

APPENDIX

FOR VIOLET

ABOUT THE AUTHOR

Angela McAllister is the author of more than 80 books for children of all ages. Her books have been adapted for the stage, translated into more than 20 languages, and have won several awards.

ABOUT THE ILLUSTRATOR

Originally hailing from Romania, Aitch's tactile, folky illustrations are inspired by her love of travel and nature. With mediums as diverse as textiles and watercolour, her dreamy characters hide among bold blooms and retain a strong sense of her Romanian heritage.

ACKNOWLEDGEMENTS

With thanks to Luke and Eleanor Farmer, Clare Faull and Sally Brown for their story suggestions and Sandra Leonard for sharing tales from her Mexican childhood – A.M.

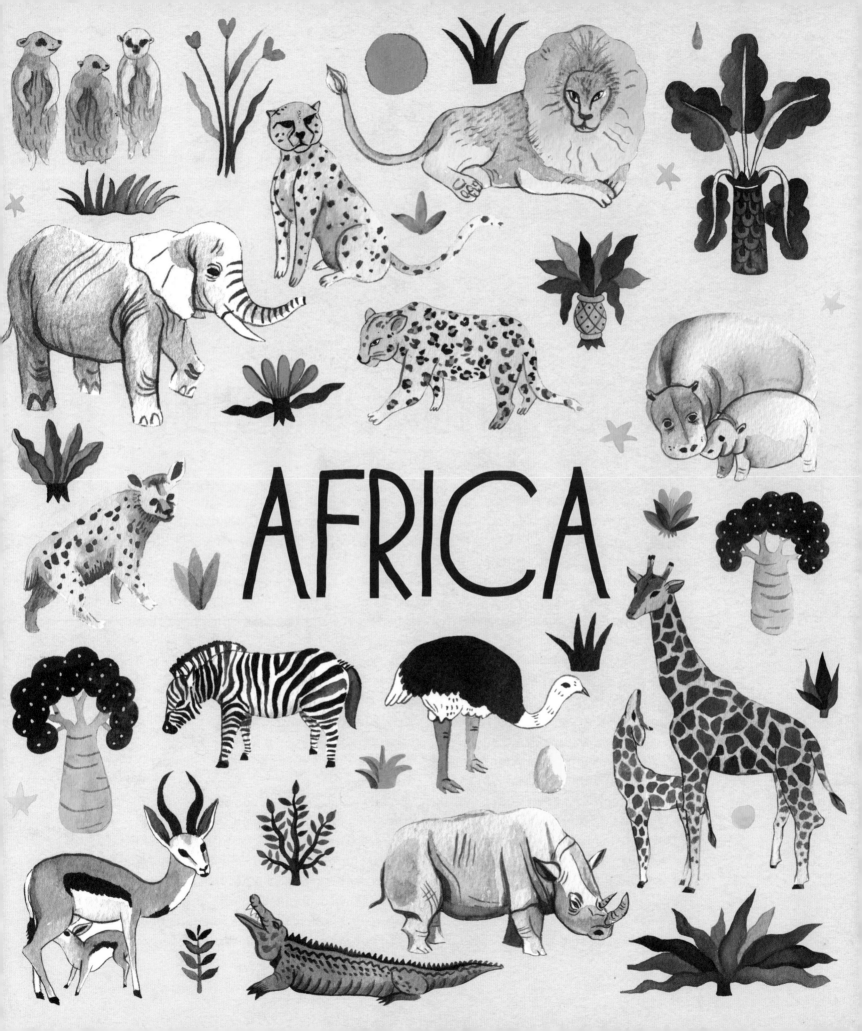

AFRICA

AFRICA
A STORY
FROM KENYA

THE TEN LITTLE OSTRICHES

Ostrich was very proud of her ten new chicks. All day she preened them and fussed over them, and told them how perfect they were. "You may be little fluff balls now," she said, "but remember, you are fine ostriches and when you grow up you'll have beautiful feathers and run as fast as the wind."

One morning, Ostrich went to find food for the chicks. She wasn't gone long, but when she returned they had disappeared. Ostrich searched among the bushes, calling for her lost chicks, but they were nowhere to be found. Then, to her horror, she saw Lion's paw prints beside those of their tiny feet.

"Oh no," she cried. "My poor little ones!" Ostrich followed the tracks to Lion's den. There, she saw her ten chicks nestled in Lion's arms.

Ostrich stepped forward bravely. "Give me back my chicks!" she demanded.

Lion stared at her and smiled. "What can you mean?" she purred softly. "All I have are my own cubs." And she nuzzled the ten fluffy chicks with her whiskery nose.

Ostrich was amazed at Lion's words. "Those aren't your cubs," she said indignantly. "They're ostriches – and they're mine!"

"I think you'll find that you're mistaken," growled Lion. "Anyone can see they are ten perfect lion cubs. If you don't believe me, fetch the other animals and ask them."

Ostrich flapped her wings helplessly. "I can't rescue those poor chicks on my own," she thought, so she hurried away to fetch the other animals. She found Zebra and Antelope, Wildebeest, Giraffe and Baboon, who all listened to her story and agreed to meet her at Lion's den later that day. Then Mongoose came along. When she heard about Ostrich's problem Mongoose thought for a while. "I think I can help you," she said, "but first there is something you must do."

"Of course," said Ostrich. "I'll do anything to get my poor little chicks back."

"Near Lion's den there's a huge anthill," said Mongoose. "You must dig a hole under it, with an entrance at the front and an exit at the back, and then wait for the other animals to arrive."

Ostrich found the anthill and did exactly as Mongoose instructed. The other animals soon arrived and stood before Lion's den.

"There," said Ostrich, "look at those little chicks with their beautiful beaks and long necks. Tell Lion who they belong to."

The animals stared at the ten fluffy chicks and then they looked at Lion. Slowly, Lion stood up. She stretched her claws and yawned, baring her sharp white teeth.

Zebra shuffled his hooves uneasily. "Well, um… in my opinion… it's plain to see that they're lion cubs," he said.

"Yes, no mistake," stuttered Antelope. "Definitely not ostriches."

"Lion cubs, without doubt," mumbled Wildebeest. Giraffe and Baboon nodded in agreement.

Ostrich couldn't believe her ears. Then Mongoose jumped up. "What nonsense!" she cried. "Have you ever seen a mother with hair and a baby with feathers?"

Lion fixed her eyes on Mongoose and snarled angrily, but Mongoose only stepped a little closer. "We all know those are chicks, not cubs, and they belong to Ostrich," she said. "Lion is a thief!" With that, Mongoose spun around and scooted towards the anthill.

Lion roared with fury and leapt after her, but Mongoose dived into the hole Ostrich had made just in time. At once, Ostrich rushed into the den and gathered up her ten little chicks. However, Lion didn't twitch a whisker. She stood looking into the anthill and didn't notice Mongoose run straight out of the back exit.

Quietly, all the animals crept away. Ostrich led her ten little chicks home and they never tired of hearing the story of that day when Lion was left staring into an empty hole.

AFRICA
A ZULU STORY

WHY THE CHEETAH'S CHEEKS ARE STAINED WITH TEARS

One morning, a lazy hunter sat under a tree, watching a herd of springbok graze nearby. He couldn't be bothered to hunt that day, but before long, he noticed a cheetah approach the herd.

The hunter watched the cheetah creep through the grass, her eyes fixed on a young springbok who'd strayed away from the rest of the herd. Suddenly, she sprang forwards, and ran so fast that her paws hardly touched the ground. Before the springbok could escape, she was upon it.

The cheetah took her prize to a patch of shade where her three hungry cubs were waiting.

"If only I had someone to hunt like that for me," thought the hunter. This gave him an idea. He knew that cheetahs never attacked men, so he decided to steal a cub and train it.

The hunter waited until the mother cheetah went off for a drink at the waterhole and then took his chance. He crept up to the patch of shade where she'd left her cubs and looked down at them. "Which one shall I choose?" he asked himself. Unable to decide which cub to take, he stole all three.

When the cheetah returned and found her cubs gone, she cried in despair. All night she cried and all the following day, until her tears made dark stains down her cheeks.

An old man who knew the ways of the animals came to ask what was wrong. When he heard what had happened, he went at once to tell the elders of the village.

"This hunter is not just a thief," said the elders angrily, "he has broken the traditions of our tribe and dishonoured us – a hunter must use only his own strength and skill." So they banished him from the village.

The old man gathered up the stolen cubs and returned them to their mother. But, since then, her tear stains appear on every cheetah's face, as a reminder that hunters should respect traditional ways.

WHY HIPPO LIVES IN WATER

Tortoise was very happy moving slowly. He didn't want to swing like Monkey or run like Cheetah. He enjoyed having a good look at the world as he plodded steadily here and there, taking his time.

However, there was one problem with being slow. Tortoise couldn't easily escape from danger. Whenever he took a walk, he had to keep an eye out for trouble – and the worst trouble for Tortoise was Hippo, who lived nearby.

Hippo had enormous, heavy feet and he also had seven wives. Together that made thirty-two enormous, heavy feet, which were very dangerous whenever they came tramping towards Tortoise.

So far, Tortoise had managed to avoid being stamped on by Hippo and his wives, although he'd had a few near misses, but he feared that his luck wouldn't last forever.

There seemed to be nothing Tortoise could do about this, until one day Hippo gave a big feast for everyone. Tortoise arrived last so that he didn't get trodden on. When Hippo looked at all the delicious food that his seven wives had prepared he felt mighty hungry.

As everyone was about to sit down to eat he said, "Friends, you have come to eat at my table, but none of you know my name."

The guests looked at each other in surprise – it was true, none of them knew Hippo's name.

"Well," said Hippo, "if you cannot tell me my name, then you cannot eat at my table!"

The guests shook their heads sadly and turned to go.

But just as greedy Hippo sat down to eat, Tortoise spoke up. "What will you do if one of us tells you your name?" he asked.

Hippo smiled to himself, knowing that only his wives knew his name.

"We shall have another feast in seven days' time," he said. "If anyone can tell me

my name then, I will do whatever they ask!" And he tucked into his enormous meal, pleased with how clever he was.

Tortoise made his way slowly home, thinking up a plan.

The next day, Hippo and his wives walked down to the river, as they loved the water and bathed every morning. Tortoise usually kept out of the way, but this particular morning he hid in the bushes and watched them walk past.

When they were all in the water, Tortoise crept into the middle of the path and dug a hole. Then he hid in the bushes again.

Hippo finished his bath and started off home, with his wives trailing behind. Tortoise waited until the last two wives stepped out of the river and then he half-buried himself in the hole, with his shell sticking out.

When the two wives came along, one of them knocked her foot against Tortoise's shell. "Oh, Istantim, my husband," she cried, "I have hurt my foot!"

Tortoise didn't wait for Hippo to return, he crept slowly away, grinning to himself.

A few days later, everyone gathered for Hippo's second feast. Once more, Hippo asked if anybody knew his name.

"I do," said Tortoise. The guests made way for him to step forwards. "Your name is Istantim!" he announced to everyone.

Everyone cheered. "Now you must keep your promise, Hippo," they said.

Hippo had to agree. "What would you like me to do, Tortoise?" he asked.

Tortoise smiled. "I'd like you and your wives to live in the river, then I can walk on the land without danger," he said.

So, after the feast, Hippo did just that and he has lived happily in the river ever since.

AFRICA
A STORY
FROM GHANA

ANANSE AND THE PYTHON

There was once a village in Ashanti with a big problem – an enormous python had come to live in the riverbank nearby. The python had a huge appetite, which he satisfied by eating the village goats and sheep.

The people of the village were afraid of the enormous python and worried that they would soon go hungry themselves, but nobody could think of a way to get rid of him, so they called on the Sky God for help.

When the Sky God heard about their problem he shook his head. "I cannot judge what to do," he said, "for the python is also one of my creatures."

"Then who can help us?" asked the villagers.

"Go and see Ananse," said the Sky God. "He's always boasting about how wise he is and I'm tired of hearing it. If he can prove his wisdom by getting rid of the python then I will reward him, but if he fails I will punish him for his bragging."

The villagers thanked the Sky God and went to Ananse's house.

Ananse was very pleased to hear that the Sky God had sent them. "I am, indeed, extremely wise," he said. "Whatever your problem, I will solve it." So the villagers told him about the enormous python.

"That is a terrible problem, my friends," said Ananse with a frown, "but not difficult for someone as wise as me. Tell me, how long is this python?"

"Longer than your house, Ananse," said one of the villagers.

"Longer than your house and the yard," said another.

"As long as your house and the yard and the house next door!" said another, and everyone nodded in agreement.

Ananse smiled to himself, then he made a solemn promise. "I, Kwaku Ananse, will use

my great wisdom to save you from the enormous python. But first I will need three things – a dish of mashed yam, a bowl of palm oil and a basket of eggs."

The villagers agreed to bring Ananse what he asked for, but as they walked away they worried that his wisdom might not be enough to save him from the huge appetite of the enormous python.

The next morning, Ananse went into the forest and chopped down a tall, straight tree. He tied it up with creepers and called his family to help him tug it down to the riverbank. There, he found the villagers waiting with a dish of mashed yam, a bowl of palm oil and a basket of eggs.

"Now hurry away," whispered Ananse urgently. "I need silence for my great wisdom to work." The villagers said a sad farewell to Ananse, fearing that they might never see him again, and left him alone.

As soon as they were gone, Ananse sat down beside the python's hole and started up a conversation with himself.

"This is a rare creature," he said. "I've heard he is the biggest, most beautiful python in the world."

The python inched a little closer to the entrance of his hole to listen.

"That's a lie," scoffed Ananse in a deep, gruff voice. "He's nothing special. Why, he couldn't even swallow a piglet!"

"It's not true," continued Ananse as himself. "He's an enormous fellow. He could swallow a whole herd of goats if he wanted to. The villagers should be proud to have him as a neighbour and bring him gifts of food, like me."

"Who would want a python as a friend?" the gruff voice said scornfully. "He's just a common old snake in the mud."

Then the python heard a thump and a scuffle and the sound of feet running away.

"Good riddance!" exclaimed Ananse. "If only the python knew how I had defended his honour. I'd like to give him this gift of mashed yam and palm oil and eggs."

At this offer of his favourite food the python slithered out of his hole, right at Ananse's feet. The sight of the python's powerful body and greedy eyes filled Ananse with dread, but he gathered all his courage and pretended not to be afraid.

"Good day, friend," said Ananse. "I've brought you a gift."

The python coiled himself around the dish and the bowl and the basket and devoured every morsel inside.

"Delicious!" he hissed. "Thank you for defending me."

"That's nothing," said Ananse. "Anyone can see you must be the biggest, most beautiful python in the world."

"In the whole world?" said the python.

"Most definitely," insisted Ananse. "In fact, I brought along this tree to prove to

everyone that it's the truth. If you wish, I can measure you with it?"

"How is it done?" asked the python.

"Just lie alongside and I'll take a measurement," explained Ananse. "When the villagers see proof of your enormous size they will all honour you with delicious food, just as I have done."

The python, feeling well fed and pleased with himself, slid his enormous body alongside the tree trunk. "It's about time I got the admiration I deserve," he murmured to himeslf.

"Now, I need to tie you to the tree, to make sure you are stretched out to your full length," said Ananse. "Then we shall see exactly how magnificent you are." And he tied the python to the tree, from head to tail, counting aloud as he went.

It wasn't until Ananse pulled the last

knot tight that the python realised he was caught. All he could do was hiss angrily at being tricked.

"You may be magnificent," laughed Ananse, "but you're not welcome here!" And he shouted for the villagers, who came running. To their amazement, instead of finding Ananse inside the python, they found him sitting on top of it!

With great relief, they carried the python far away from the village, so that he wouldn't bother them again.

"You have earned your reward, Ananse," said the Sky God, reluctantly. "I shall make sure that the python does not return, and you shall have a pot of wisdom."

Then, in his frustration, he flung the pot of wisdom down so hard that it nearly split Ananse in two, giving him a narrow waist for evermore.

AFRICA
A STORY FROM NIGERIA

THE ANTS AND THE TREASURE

In a village in Africa there lived a poor man who was very kind to animals and birds. He grew a little food, which he shared with his parrot, and every morning he sprinkled some crumbs outside for the ants.

The ants were grateful and showed their thanks by not eating anything in the poor man's vegetable patch.

On the other side of the village lived a miser who'd collected a large pile of gold coins by tricking people out of their money. He kept his hoard of treasure in a hut, which he guarded day and night.

The miser was selfish and cruel. He threw stones at any animals or birds who came near his hut and crushed ants beneath his feet.

The ants tried to think of a way to punish the cruel miser.

"Isn't it a pity that the man who is our friend is so poor and the man who is our enemy is so rich?" said their king. This gave the ants an idea.

They dug a tunnel between the miser's hut and the poor man's house. Then they carried some gold coins along the tunnel and left them by the poor man's bed.

The poor man was amazed when he woke up and found a heap of gold glittering on the floor. "This must be a gift from the gods," he thought happily and he put the coins under his bed.

Meanwhile, the miser was alarmed to discover that some of his treasure was missing. He couldn't understand how anyone could have entered the hut while he'd been keeping watch.

That night, the ants carried more gold coins along the tunnel to the poor man's house. As there was no more room under the bed the poor man covered the pile of coins with a cloth.

The miser was angry to discover that more of his treasure was gone, but still he had no idea what had happened.

On the third night the ants carried all the remaining coins to the poor man's house. As before, he thanked the gods and covered the coins with the cloth.

The miser shouted with rage when he found the hut was empty. His neighbours came to see what was wrong.

"There must be magic at work," they said when they heard what had happened. But when the miser searched the hut he found the tunnel.

"Aha!" he cried. "If we find the other end of this tunnel we'll have the thief!"

Everyone in the village joined in the search. Before long the other end of the tunnel was found in the poor man's house, along with the gold coins beneath the cloth.

"I'm not a thief," protested the poor man. "I thought this treasure was a gift from the gods. How could I crawl through a tiny tunnel like that?"

"You must have made yourself small with magic!" said the miser.

The villagers locked the poor man in a hut. "We'll decide your punishment tomorrow," they said.

The ants were upset that their plan had caused such trouble. The king called for all his people to help rescue their friend.

Thousands and thousands of ants arrived and, while the villagers slept, they ate the whole hut – roof, walls and door.

In the morning, the villagers looked at the remains of the hut and shook their heads. "The gods must have decided this punishment," they said. "Ants have eaten the hut and the prisoner!"

The ants smiled to themselves. Only they knew that their friend had escaped from the hut, fetched his parrot and the gold still beneath his bed and walked away from the village to start a new life.

AFRICA

AFRICA
A STORY FROM WEST AFRICA

THE LEOPARD AND THE RAM

Ram wanted a good place to build himself a new house. Then, one day as he was exploring the forest, he came to a clearing that seemed the perfect spot. "Here is a light, dry place, with plenty of wood to build my house," said Ram to himself. "I shall fetch my tools and begin work right away."

While Ram went home to fetch his tools, Leopard arrived at the clearing and had exactly the same idea. "This is the perfect place to build a new house," he said to himself and he started to gather the wood he needed.

When Ram returned, he was surprised to see a great pile of wood had been gathered for his house. "There must be a kind spirit in this forest," he thought and he got to work.

The following evening, when Leopard arrived, he was astonished to find that his house was already begun. "It must be the work of a good spirit," he thought, and he continued where the work had left off.

They carried on this way, with Ram building in the day and Leopard working at night, never seeing each other, until the house was finished. Then they both arrived to move in. At first, Ram and Leopard were astonished to learn the truth about their fine house, but after a friendly discussion they decided to live in it together.

All went well. Ram and Leopard both had sons who played happily together while their parents went hunting.

After a while, Leopard noticed that Ram caught just as much game as he did, even though he had no claws or sharp teeth. He was curious to know how it was done, so he asked his son to find out from the young ram.

The next day, while their parents were away, the little leopard asked the young ram how his father hunted.

"I'll show you how he does it if you show me how your father hunts," said the young ram, and the little leopard agreed. They fetched two large pieces of plantain stem and went into the woods.

First, the little leopard propped up his piece of plantain. Fixing his eye upon it, he moved from left to right, bowing and peeping, just like his father did. Then he sprang forwards and pounced on it.

"Bravo!" cried his friend.

"Your turn," said the little leopard. The young ram put his piece of plantain in position and then backed away from it.

When he was ready, he took aim, charged and tore the plantain to shreds. "That's how it's done!" he said.

That evening, the little leopard told his father what he'd learned. "Beware," he said, "if you ever see Ram go backwards, then you know he's about to charge."

The leopard thanked his son for the information and good advice.

A few days later it rained, making the floor of the house very slippery. Leopard invited Ram to share a meal with him, as usual, but as Ram came through the door he slid backwards on the wet floor.

Remembering what his son had told him about Ram's hunting technique, Leopard feared that Ram was about to charge at him. "Run!" he cried to his family and they fled all together, out of the house, across the clearing and away into the woods.

Ram and his son called them back, but Leopard refused to return, and from that day on, all leopards have lived in the forest, while rams have remained at home.

AFRICA
FROM
EAST AFRICA

WHY THE WARTHOG IS UGLY

Warthog was once a handsome beast who was very proud of his fine looks. He loved to admire himself and often boasted about his beauty to the other animals of the savannah. He was so vain and rude that nobody liked him at all.

Warthog had made his home in an abandoned aardvark hole, which he'd enlarged to make a comfy den. It was also a safe place to hide whenever his rude remarks got him into trouble.

One morning, Warthog went out to look for some breakfast. He didn't notice Porcupine, who'd been awake all night and was searching for somewhere to sleep.

As soon as Warthog was out of sight, Porcupine slipped into Warthog's den and scuttled down to his cosy bed for a nap.

Meanwhile, Warthog enjoyed a good meal, followed by a drink at the waterhole and a long wallow in the mud. Then along came Lion. Warthog was feeling so pleased with himself that he couldn't resist telling Lion how scruffy his mane looked, compared to his own fine bristles.

"I'll teach you not to be rude to me," roared Lion angrily.

Warthog realised he was in trouble. He clambered out of the water as fast as he could and ran towards home with Lion at his heels.

As Warthog came in sight of his den, he breathed a sigh of relief. He shot inside, thinking he was safe. Unaware that there was a visitor inside, he crashed straight into Porcupine and got a face-full of sharp quills.

Out he came again, howling with pain.

"Let that be a lesson to you," said Lion as he walked away.

It took Warthog a long time to remove Porcupine's quills. None of the other animals would help because he'd been rude to them all. To his dismay, his swollen face was left covered in ugly warts and bumps.

From that day, Warthog lost his handsomeness – and always entered his den backwards!

ASIA

ASIA
A STORY FROM INDIA

THE ELEPHANT
AND THE BLIND MEN

There was once a wise man who travelled the world on a fine elephant. One evening, while looking for somewhere to stay for the night, he came upon a house that was owned by six brothers.

The wise man knocked on the door and asked the brothers if they would be kind enough to provide him with a bed and somewhere for his elephant to sleep.

The brothers looked puzzled. "What is an elephant?" they asked.

"You've never seen one?" exclaimed the wise man. "Then prepare to be amazed!"

But the sun had already slipped below the horizon and there was no moon that night, so the wise man said to the brothers, "It's dark now. Let us sleep tonight and then you shall see how magnificent an elephant is in the morning."

The brothers smiled. "We are all blind," they told the wise man. "The darkness is nothing to us. Come, lead us to this magnificent thing that you call an elephant immediately, as we are eager to know all about it!"

Then one of the brothers fetched a lantern, which they kept for guests, and the wise man led them outside to where his elephant was standing, nibbling the leaves of a tree. The wise man stroked the gentle elephant's head.

"Here, I have brought six new friends to admire you," he said.

The six blind brothers gathered around the elephant. The first one stepped forward and put out his hand. He touched the elephant's leg. "Aha, it's like the pillar of a building," he said.

The second brother took hold of the elephant's tail. "No," he said, "it's like a thick rope."

The third brother reached out and felt the elephant's trunk. "Not at all," he remarked. "It resembles a thick branch with rough bark."

The fourth brother brushed his hand against the elephant's ear. "What are you all talking about?" he said, crossly. "I say it feels like a leather apron."

The fifth brother bumped into the elephant's belly. "You're all talking complete nonsense!" he insisted. "I can tell you that an elephant is obviously like a large tent!"

The sixth brother reached up and grasped the elephant's tusk. "No, I say you're all wrong, it's like a curved pipe."

The blind brothers began to argue fiercely among themselves. Each one was sure that he understood exactly what an elephant was like.

"How can it be like a tent when it swings like a rope?" said one brother.

"It can't be like an apron when it's hard like a pipe!" said another.

"I'm the eldest and I say it's like a pillar, not a rough branch!" said a third.

The wise man sat in the lantern light and smiled quietly to himself.

After a little while, he interrupted their quarrel. "Friends," he said, "there is no need to fight among yourselves. You are each right in what you have discovered. But you are all wrong to think that what you know is the whole truth.

"An elephant is made up of many parts. If you want to discover how magnificent he really is, I suggest you listen to what each of your brothers has learned and has to say on the matter!"

Then the six brothers felt ashamed of their outburst and apologised to each other.

"Forgive us," said the eldest brother. "We may not yet understand the magnificence of the elephant, but we all recognise the words of a wise man."

ASIA

23

ASIA
A STORY
FROM JAPAN

THE WHITE BUTTERFLY

Old Takahama lived in a little house beside the cemetery of the temple of Sozanji.

He was always kind to his neighbours, who were very fond of him, although they thought it strange that Takahama had never married, or even looked for a wife.

One summer's day, old Takahama felt unwell. He sent for his brother's widow.

The widow came and brought her son, who loved his uncle dearly.

"I know I have not long to live," sighed old Takahama.

"Then we shall take care of you," promised the widow.

The following day, as Takahama was sleeping, a white butterfly flew into his room and settled on the pillow, beside his head.

The boy gently drove the white butterfly away, but moments later it returned. The same thing happened again and again, until the boy finally chased the white butterfly out into the garden.

He followed the beautiful creature into the cemetery, where she fluttered around an old tomb and then disappeared. The boy read the name inscribed there: 'Akiko'.

Although the tomb was over fifty years old, someone had cleared the moss away and laid white roses before it.

The boy returned to the house, to find that his uncle had just died. He told his mother what he'd seen at the cemetery and, to his surprise, she smiled.

"When your uncle was young, he loved a beautiful girl called Akiko," she explained.

"Sadly, Akiko died before their wedding day. Takahama vowed he would never marry anyone else and built this house by the cemetery so that he could always pray at her grave.

"Every day, in sun, rain or snow, he swept er tomb and left flowers for Akiko." Then the boy saw that his uncle was peacefully smiling too; for the white butterfly was Akiko and they were together at last.

ASIA
A STORY FROM TIBET

THE COUNTRY OF THE MICE

Once, there was a country ruled over by a good king, in which there lived a great number of mice. The mice usually had plenty to eat, as they collected grain that was left lying in the fields after the farmers had harvested their crops. But one year, the harvest was bad and they couldn't gather enough grain to fill their stores for the winter. So one of the mice put on his finest clothes and went to see the king, to ask for his help.

When the king heard that a mouse wished to see him he was very amused and ordered that he be shown into the throne room. It was the custom for a visitor to give the king a silk scarf, so the mouse solemnly presented him with a little silk thread.

"Thank you, Brother Mouse," said the king. "How can I help you?"

"Your Majesty," said the mouse, "the harvest has been poor this year, so the mice don't have enough food for the winter. If you lend us some grain, I promise that we will repay you at the next harvest."

"How much do you need?" asked the king.

"One of your big barns should be enough," replied the mouse.

"But how will you carry it all?"

"Leave it to us," said the mouse. "If you give us the grain, we will carry it away."

The king admired the little mouse's boldness, so he ordered his guards to open the doors of a big barn full of barley.

That night, the mouse summoned all the mice in the country. Hundreds and thousands came and each one took away as many grains as he could carry; in his mouth, on his back and curled up in his tail.

In the morning, the king was very impressed to hear that not a single grain of barley was left in the barn.

ASIA

Thanks to his kindness, the mice had plenty to eat all winter. Next harvest, they repaid the loan by filling the king's barn with grain, just as the mouse had promised. "I see they are trustworthy as well as clever," said the king to himself.

A few months later, the ruler of the neighbouring country declared war on the country of the mice. He brought his powerful army down to the river, which was the border between the two countries, and prepared to invade.

Once more, the mouse went to the palace. He found the king looking very gloomy. "Your Majesty," said the mouse, "last time I came here you did my people a great favour. Now I have come to offer you our help to defeat your enemy."

Although his troubles were heavy, the king smiled. He lifted the little mouse onto his hand. "Thank you, Brother Mouse," he said. "But how can you help? Our neighbour's army is ten times greater than ours."

"Last time you doubted that we could carry away a barn full of grain, or repay your loan," said the mouse. "But we did both. If you trust us again then I promise we will get rid of this invading army."

The king had learned to trust the mice and so he agreed. "What do you need for this task?" he asked.

"A hundred thousand cakes of dried yak dung," said the mouse, "to be laid along the riverbank." The king was puzzled by this request, but ordered it to be done at once.

The following evening, all the mice of the country gathered at the riverbank. They put the cakes of yak dung in the water and climbed on board. Then they pushed off from the riverbank and sailed to the other side.

The enemy's soldiers were all asleep, some in their tents and some outside, with their weapons beside them. Silently, the mice scattered throughout the camp. Each one

ASIA

began to nibble whatever he could find; some nibbled the strings of the soldiers' bows or the slings of their muskets, some the fuses, others bit their clothes and pigtails, some chewed the tents and sacks of food, tearing everything to shreds. Then, without a sound, they sailed back across the river, leaving every man still fast asleep.

The next morning, when the enemy soldiers awoke they were alarmed to find their clothes in tatters, their pigtails cut off, their tents destroyed and their weapons ruined. In great confusion, the men started to accuse each other and a huge argument began.

At that moment, the king of the country of the mice ordered one of his men to blow a bugle. The enemy thought it was under attack! The soldiers were too disorganised to defend themselves, so they turned and fled in a panic, without a shot being fired.

The king thanked the mice. "The whole country is grateful for your bravery," he said. "What can I do to repay you?"

"We mice have to face two dangers," said the mouse. "Many of our burrows are near the river and when the water overflows it floods our nests. If you build a dam along the bank then we will be safe." The king agreed to do so. "And what is the second danger?" he asked.

"Cats, Your Majesty!" said the mouse.

"Of course!" The king laughed. "From this day forward, I forbid anyone in my kingdom to keep a cat." And so the mice returned to their homes, to live without any fear of danger.

Then the king sent a herald across the river with a message for the ruler of that country. "Today you have been defeated by my mice alone," he said. "But if you try to invade again, I will send my dogs; and if they don't succeed, I shall send the wild beasts of my country."

When the king's enemy heard these words he shuddered with fear. "If the mice of that country are so fearsome, then we must sign a treaty of peace at once," he said. And that is exactly what they did.

ASIA
A STORY FROM INDIA

THE FARMER AND THE MULE

One morning, a farmer heard a strange noise coming from his well. He peered over the edge and saw, to his dismay, that his old mule had fallen inside.

The farmer felt sorry for the mule, who was stamping and braying in distress, but he didn't know what to do about it.

He went next door to ask for his neighbour's help.

"Well, we can't reach him," said the neighbour. "You'd better put him out of his misery."

The farmer sadly agreed. "This dry well is no use anyway," he said. "We should fill it with earth and bury the poor old mule."

So they fetched their shovels and began to throw earth into the well.

When the first shovel of earth hit the mule's back he kicked his hooves crossly. With the second shovel of earth, he realised that he was not going to be rescued and began to panic.

Then he heard the cockerel crow in the yard.

The mule calmed himself. "I'm not just going to stand here and be buried at the bottom of this well," he thought, and so he shook the earth off his back, stamped it down and stood on top of the pile.

"Shake it off and step up!" he told himself.

Although he was in a tight spot, afraid and bruised from his fall, the old mule started shaking off the earth heaped upon him and stepping onto the pile.

"Don't give up, shake it off and step up!" he repeated to himself. Slowly, little by little, he began to rise…

The farmer and his neighbour worked long and hard trying to fill the well that day, but they dropped their shovels and danced with joy when the stubborn old mule stepped right out in front of their very eyes!

ASIA
A STORY FROM INDIA

THE LION AND THE CLEVER JACKALS

D eep in the jungle, there lived a fierce lion. Every morning, he would stand at the entrance of his den and roar a terrible roar that echoed through the jungle. When the other animals heard this terrifying sound they would run around in alarm, and then the lion would leap out and pounce on them.

He was so powerful that nobody ever escaped his mighty claws.

This went on for a long, long time until, at last, there were no living creatures left in the jungle, except two little Jackals.

The little jackals had no rest. They had to keep on the move and use all their cleverness to avoid being ambushed by the lion.

"I'm sure he will catch us soon," sighed the youngest jackal.

"Don't be afraid," said his sister, "I'll take care of you. Just keep close to me."

Meanwhile, the lion grew very hungry and very cross.

At last, the youngest jackal felt he could run no more. "I'm so tired," he said. "If only there was another way to save ourselves."

His sister felt sorry for him. "I have an idea," she said, "follow me just a little further." And, to the youngest jackal's astonishment, his sister walked right up to the lion's den. "Be brave," she whispered to her brother, "and all will be well."

When the lion saw the jackals approaching he shook his mane and roared. "Come and be eaten!" he said. "I've had no dinner for three days and you've made me run all over the jungle after you."

The youngest jackal shook with terror, but his sister took a step forward. "Oh Mighty Lion," she said, "we would have come to be eaten sooner, but there is a much bigger lion in this jungle who has been chasing us away."

29

ASIA

"What do you mean?" growled the lion. "There is no other lion in this jungle but me!"

"We have seen him with our own eyes," said the jackal. "His face is like a flaming fire, his roar is like thunder and he has the strength of ten lions."

"Impossible!" said the lion angrily. "There is no beast mightier than me! Take me to him. I will show him who is the strongest."

The jackal beckoned to her brother and they set off through the jungle with the lion following.

When they came to a large well, the jackal stopped. She pointed at the water, pretending that she was too afraid to look into it herself. "There," she said, "that is where the great lion lives."

The lion stared down into the well and thought he saw another lion glaring up at him. He growled and shook his mane.

To his annoyance, the other lion did exactly the same back!

"See how fierce and powerful he is," said the jackal. "Surely no one can defeat him?"

"How dare you say such a thing? This imposter is nothing compared to me!" snarled the lion, and his reflection snarled back at him.

He opened his jaws and bared his teeth, and the other lion did exactly the same. At this, the lion flew into a rage.

"This is my jungle!" he roared and he leapt at his reflection, plunging with a loud splash into the cold, deep water of the well.

The little jackals cheered and danced with glee.

"Get me out!" spluttered the lion, trying to grasp the steep sides with his paws.

"You'll pay for this with your scrawny bones!" growled the lion.

But the two jackals scampered away, happy that the jungle was safe at last.

ASIA

URASHIMA AND THE TURTLE

Many years ago, on an island in Japan, there lived an old fisherman and his son, Urashima. The old fisherman had taught his son all the skills of the sea and Urashima loved nothing better than to spend the day in his boat, rocking on the great green waves.

One day, when he was out fishing, Urashima felt something heavy on the end of his line. He tugged the catch out of the water and, to his surprise, a young turtle dropped into his boat. Urashima unhooked her gently from the fishing line. "Don't be afraid," he said. "I've heard that a turtle can live for a thousand years. I will set you free to enjoy your long life." Then Urashima lifted the turtle over the edge of the boat, and released her into the sea, Then she disappeared under the waves.

The following day, while Urashima was out fishing, the turtle reappeared beside his boat. To his astonishment, she spoke.

"I have come to thank you for saving my life, Urashima," she said. "Would you like to see the palace of the Dragon King?" Urashima had heard many tales about the Dragon King's palace under the sea.

"Yes," he answered excitedly, "but how can I travel beneath the waves?"

"Sit on my back," said the turtle, "and your wish will come true." Before his eyes she grew, until she was big enough for him to sit comfortably on her shell. Then the turtle dived beneath the waves and Urashima found himself riding through the ocean, marvelling at the curious creatures of the sea.

The turtle swam on. Urashima was so enchanted by everything he saw that he had no idea how long they travelled. At last, they came to a garden of pink coral, where the trees glittered with jewels. The turtle stopped before a shimmering gate of golden seaweed and told Urashima that there they must say goodbye. "The Dragon Princess, Otohime, is waiting to greet you," she said.

ASIA

Wide-eyed, Urashima stepped through the golden gate and found himself in front of a gleaming palace made of shells and pearls. There to greet him was a beautiful girl, with skin as white as blossom, hair as black as night and eyes as bright as flecks of sunlight on the waves.

"Welcome, Urashima," she said. "I am the Dragon Princess, Otohime."

Urashima was so overcome that he couldn't speak. He followed the princess into the palace, where her attendants clothed him in robes of silk. "The turtle you set free was my handmaiden," said Otohime. "She told me about your kind heart, so I wished to meet you. Will you stay and keep me company for a while?"

Urashima gazed at Otohime. He forgot about his boat. He forgot about his old father at home. "Yes," he said. "I will stay with you."

Then Urashima and Otohime shared a banquet of delicious food and were entertained by fine fish musicians. Afterwards, she showed him the most precious treasures in the palace.

From that day forward, Urashima and Otohime were always together. They travelled far and wide throughout her father's watery kingdom exploring the fabulous seabed and, before long, their hearts were full of love for each other. The Dragon King gave his blessing for their wedding and all the creatures of the ocean came to celebrate their joyful marriage.

Urashima was so happy, he didn't count the days and months that passed. But one afternoon, a dark shape glided far above his head, like a rain cloud crossing the sky.

"Don't be alarmed," said Otohime, "it's only a fishing boat passing overhead."

At these words, Urashima suddenly remembered his own boat and his old father, waiting for him at home.

ASIA

"What is wrong?" asked Otohime.

"I must go home and tell my father all that has happened," said Urashima. "He will be worried about me."

The princess was dismayed. She tried to persuade Urashima not to go. "If you leave me you will never come back!" she cried and her eyes filled with tears. But Urashima told her that he loved her dearly and would not be away for long.

"When I return we shall be together forever," he promised.

Otohime dried her eyes and fetched a little silver casket. "Take this," she told Urashima. "It will bring you home to me. But whatever happens, never open the box." Then she called the turtle to carry Urashima back to the shore.

Urashima walked up the beach grinning to himself as he thought of the good news he had to tell his father. But when he reached the place where his house should have been, he found nothing but a pile of mossy stones.

"What happened?" he cried aloud. "Father? Father?"

A man in strange clothes walked up the path. "Can I help you?" he asked.

"Where is the house that stood here?" asked Urashima.

"There hasn't been a house here for centuries," said the man. "Nobody wants to live here because of the sad story of the fisherman whose son sailed away one day and never returned."

"What happened to the old man?" asked Urashima in disbelief.

"He died three hundred years ago," said the stranger.

Urashima rushed into the village. The houses were different, but the graveyard hadn't changed. There, to his dismay, he found his father's tomb and the terrible proof of the stranger's words.

Urashima was overwhelmed with grief. "I must return to Otohime," he sighed. But when he went back to the beach, the turtle was nowhere to be seen. Urashima paced up and down the shore, calling out to his wife, but no one appeared. Then he remembered the silver casket. "Otohime promised this would bring me home," he thought desperately.

Completely forgetting the princess's warning, Urashima opened the casket. Inside was nothing but a wisp of white smoke. Suddenly, his fingers began to grow thin. His arms felt weak and his breath was short. "I'm growing old!" he gasped and Urashima knew that he would never return to the palace under the sea.

With a deep sigh, Urashima sat and gazed out across the waves. He thought of his beautiful wife and his father, waiting for him somewhere, until the silver casket fell softly from his withered hands.

ASIA

A STORY FROM CHINA

THE NODDING TIGER

A long time ago, in a village outside the walls of a great city in China, there lived a young woodcutter named T'ang and his old mother. They were very poor, but T'ang would walk up the mountain each day and cut firewood, which he sold at the market. In this way, he earned enough money to buy all the things his mother needed.

One morning, T'ang took his axe and went up the mountain as usual, but by late in the day he hadn't returned. "He should be home by now," fretted Widow T'ang, "or else he will miss the market." As night fell she was sure that some terrible fate had befallen him.

"My poor T'ang!" she cried. "My good, kind son!" She took up her stick and hobbled to her neighbour's house to beg him to look for the missing boy.

The neighbour fetched a lantern and set off along the mountain path. Half way up, he found a little pile of torn clothing spattered with blood and the woodcutter's axe lying beside it. With a heavy heart he returned to tell Widow T'ang the terrible truth – that her son had been carried off by a tiger.

Widow T'ang wept with grief. "He was my only son," she cried. "Who will take care of me now?" She was so distressed that nobody could comfort her.

However, the next day, to her neighbour's surprise, she set off down the road to the city. "Poor woman," he thought, "she has no one to support her now."

When she arrived at the city, Widow T'ang went to the court house. She sat on the steps and began to wail and cry. The Mandarin heard the old woman and called for her to be brought into the court. "What troubles you?" he asked.

Widow T'ang dried her eyes and told the Mandarin what had happened to her son. "I am old and poor, with no one to look after me now," she said. "I ask for justice. The tiger must be punished for his crime."

ASIA

The Mandarin looked at her in astonishment. "How can a tiger be brought to justice?" he exclaimed. "You ask the impossible!" At these words, Widow T'ang started wailing and howling even louder than before.

"All right, all right," said the Mandarin. "Go home and it will be done."

But the old woman knew he was just trying to get rid of her. "I won't go until I see you give the order," she said. The Mandarin, who was not unkind, took pity on the poor widow. He asked for a volunteer to arrest the tiger, but nobody came forward. However, at the back of the room, one of his assistants, a lazy man named Li-neng, was fast asleep. Just at that moment a sneeze woke him up and he jumped to his feet.

"Thank you, Li-neng," said the Mandarin, thinking he had volunteered. "You shall arrest the tiger and bring him to justice."

Widow T'ang was satisfied with this and went home. But Li-neng looked at the Mandarin in horror. Arrest a tiger? It couldn't be done!

The other assistants explained to Li-neng what had happened while he was asleep. "It must be a joke," he thought. "The Mandarin just wanted to get rid of that old woman." So the following day he reported that the tiger couldn't be found.

The Mandarin was not happy. "I gave Widow T'ang my word," he said. "You shall lose a week's pay if you don't arrest the tiger."

Li-neng saw he had no choice but to gather some hunters and go up into the mountain. They searched the hills and caves but without any success. Once more, Li-neng reported that the tiger couldn't be found.

ASIA

"Then you shall lose a month's pay," said the Mandarin and he sent him off to try again. When Li-neng returned without a tiger for the third time the Mandarin was very cross and told him he would be banished from the city unless he brought the tiger to court.

Li-neng was miserable. "Why don't you run away?" suggested the other assistants, but Li-neng shook his head.

"I can't leave my family," he said. Feeling hopeless, he went to the mountain temple to pray. "What can I do?" he sighed. "I've been given an impossible task and a terrible punishment."

Just then he heard rustling nearby. Looking up he saw a huge tiger standing at the temple gate. Li-neng was too unhappy even to feel afraid. "So," he said, "you have come to put me out of my misery!" He told the tiger about the old woman who depended on her only son, how he had lost his pay because he hadn't arrested the tiger and how he was going to be banished from his home and family. "So you might as well eat me," he said, "I have nothing to live for."

While he spoke, the tiger listened closely. Then, to Li-neng's amazement, he padded slowly towards him, picked up a rope in his mouth and hung his head. Li-neng slipped the rope around the tiger's neck and led him down the mountain.

When Li-neng brought the tiger into the courtroom everyone was filled with wonder. Widow T'ang heard the news and came at once. The tiger sat calmly in front of the Mandarin, like a huge cat.

"Tiger," said the Mandarin, "did you eat the woodcutter, T'ang?"

The tiger nodded his head.

"Justice!" cried Widow T'ang. "Give him the punishment he deserves!"

"Tiger," said the Mandarin, "this helpless old woman loved her son and has no one else to depend on. Do you promise to take the place of this woman's son and support her from now on?"

The tiger nodded his head.

"Very well then, justice is done," said the Mandarin and he ordered the tiger to be freed. Then the tiger walked out of the courtroom and went back to the mountain.

The old woman was very angry. "Whoever heard of a tiger taking the place of a son?" she cried, but there was nothing more to be done and she returned home, broken-hearted.

The next morning, she found a deer on her doorstep. Her tiger-son had begun to keep his promise. She took it to the market and sold it for lots of money. A week later, the tiger came to her door with some birds for her to sell. Widow T'ang saw that the Mandarin had acted wisely and was grateful.

The tiger grew attached to the old woman and often purred at her door, so that she would stroke him. When, at last, Widow T'ang died, the faithful tiger lay on her grave and mourned her, before vanishing into the mountains, never to be seen again.

A STORY FROM TIBET

THE LEGEND OF THE PANDA

Some say that, long, long ago, the pandas that lived in the mountains of Tibet were once as white as snow. One day, a panda cub wandered away from its parents and got a thorn stuck in its paw.

Four shepherdesses, who were watching over their flock of sheep, saw the cub cradling its paw and befriended it.

One of them gently removed the thorn and, to their delight, the cub stayed with them, eating bamboo shoots and playing happily with the lambs.

Suddenly, a leopard leapt out of the bushes to attack the panda cub.

The shepherdesses threw themselves in front of the frightened cub and grabbed sticks to beat the leopard away.

While they fought the leopard, the little cub ran home to safety. The leopard was angry at being denied his prey and so he killed the brave shepherdesses instead.

When the other pandas heard what had happened, they were deeply saddened by the news. They smeared their arms with black ashes, which was the local custom, and went to the funeral of the four shepherdesses.

That day, the pandas cried with sorrow. As they wiped the tears away, their eyes were stained with ash. The guests at the funeral wept so loudly that the pandas covered their ears, turning them black too. When the pandas comforted each other with a hug, their bodies were blackened from front to back. In honour of the brave shepherdesses, they made a vow never to wash the ash from their fur.

Then the earth shook and a great mountain rose out of the grave into the sky. The four shepherdesses were transformed into four peaks as a reminder of the sacrifice they made for the little cub, and pandas have found safety in the shepherdesses' arms ever since.

ASIA
A STORY FROM JAPAN

HOW THE JELLYFISH LOST HIS BONES

In the beginning, Jellyfish had a round shell, as white as the moon, and four legs so that he could walk along the seabed.

Sadly, he lost his fine white shell and his four strong legs by being foolish, and this is what happened.

The Kingdom of the Sea was governed by the Dragon King. One day his wife, the queen, fell ill. The Dragon King sent for the fish doctor, who examined the queen and gave her a dose of medicine. But the medicine didn't make the queen feel any better, so he gave her a pill, and when that didn't work, he tried a soothing ointment. However, despite all his remedies the queen only felt worse.

"Isn't there anything else you can do, Doctor?" asked the Dragon King.

"There is one thing that might cure the queen," said the fish doctor, "but it can't be found under the sea."

"What is it?" demanded the Dragon King impatiently.

"They say eating the liver of a monkey can sometimes cure an illness like this."

"Then we must try it right away," insisted the Dragon King. "Where can we find one?"

"Monkey Island is not far from here," said the fish doctor. "But how could any of your subjects go ashore and catch a monkey?"

The queen sighed and gave a little cough. "Send Jellyfish," she said weakly.

"Of course, my dear," exclaimed the Dragon King. "Jellyfish can walk on land. Somebody go and fetch him at once!"

Jellyfish was brought to the palace and instructed to swim to Monkey Island and catch a monkey. "We need its liver to make the queen well again," explained the fish doctor.

"How will I get the monkey to come with me?" asked Jellyfish.

"Tell him about the wonders of our kingdom under the sea," said the Dragon King, "and invite him to join us for a banquet at the Palace. He will not be able to resist such an offer."

Jellyfish promised to do what the king asked, feeling very proud to have been chosen for this important task, and he set off straightaway.

When Jellyfish reached Monkey Island he walked ashore and soon found a monkey, sitting in the branches of a persimmon tree.

"Good day, Monkey," he said. "This is a fine island."

"Yes," agreed Monkey. "It's the best place in the world."

ASIA

"Oh no," said Jellyfish. "I'm afraid you're mistaken there. The best place in the world is the kingdom of the Dragon King. Why, it's more beautiful than anything you could ever dream of."

"Is that so?" said Monkey.

"Yes," said Jellyfish. "In fact, I've been sent to invite you to a banquet at the palace, if you would like to see it."

"How would I get there?" asked Monkey.

"By taking a ride on my shell," said Jellyfish. "It isn't far."

Monkey liked the idea of a banquet, so he agreed. He slipped down from the persimmon tree and followed Jellyfish to the shore. There, he climbed onto Jellyfish's round white shell and they set off together across the sea.

After a while, Jellyfish laughed at how clever he'd been.

"What makes you laugh?" asked Monkey.

"I've tricked you, Monkey," he said.

ASIA

"The Dragon King wants your liver for the queen to eat, so she will recover from her illness," chuckled Jellyfish."

"Oh dear," sighed the monkey. "I wish you'd told me this before we left the island."

"Why would I do that?" asked Jellyfish.

"Well," said Monkey, "you see, my liver is rather heavy, so I take it out and hang it on the persimmon tree every morning. I was so excited to see your wonderful land that I'm afraid I've left it behind."

Jellyfish, who didn't know anything about monkeys or livers, wasn't sure what to do.

"Don't worry," said the monkey, "I'm sure the Dragon King won't mind and the queen will be fine without it. Let's get along to the banquet."

"No, no," said Jellyfish, "I can't bring you to the banquet without it. We'll have to go back." And with that, he turned around and swam back to Monkey Island.

As soon as they reached the island, Monkey scampered back up into his persimmon tree.

"Have you got your liver now?" called out Jellyfish.

"Yes!" laughed the monkey. "It's safe inside me and that's where it's going to stay!" At that moment the jellyfish knew that he'd been tricked.

There was nothing he could do but return to the palace and explain to the king what had happened.

When the Dragon King found out that Jellyfish had failed to bring the cure for the queen, he ordered his guards to remove Jellyfish's beautiful white shell and pull all the bones out of his legs as a punishment.

And so, the jellyfish never walked on the seabed or the shore again.

However, when the queen heard the story about how Monkey had tricked Jellyfish, she laughed so much that she felt quite better.

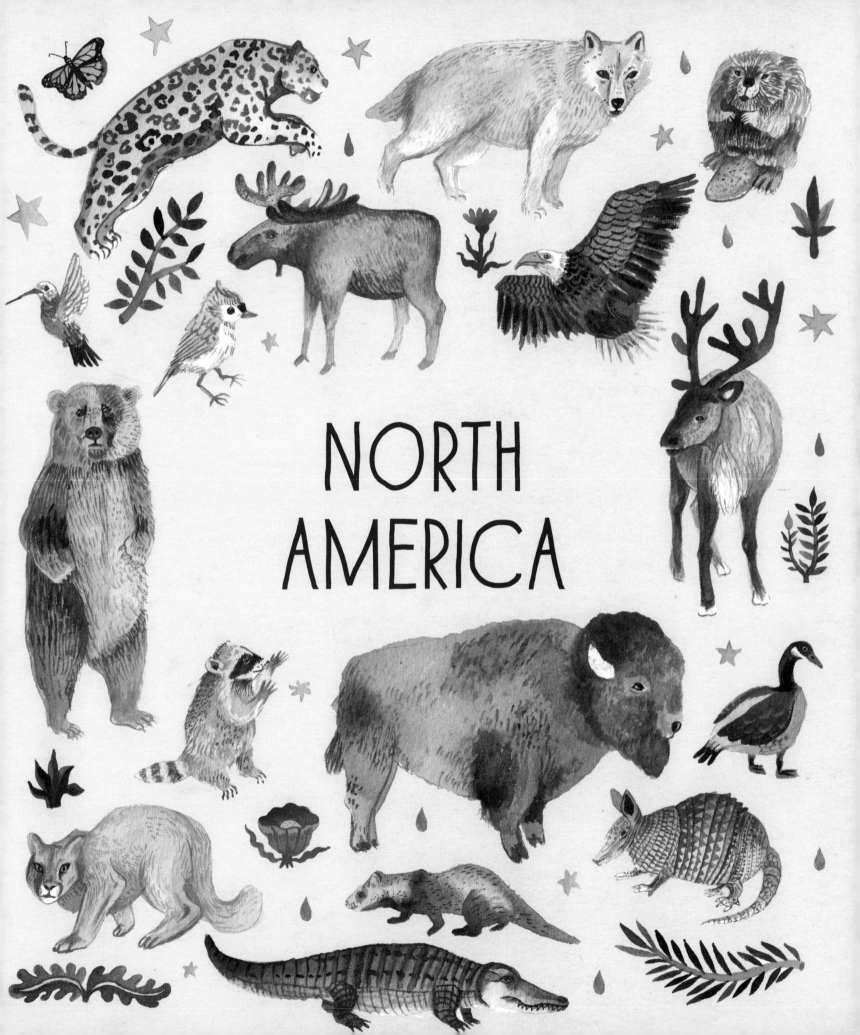

NORTH
AMERICA

NORTH AMERICA
A BLACKFOOT STORY

BUFFALO AND EAGLE WING

A long time ago, there were only tall, straight trees and bushes, with enough space between them so that a man could walk without a path, and the land was smooth under his feet, without any stones.

A great buffalo wandered across the land. He had a spirit power, which enabled him to change things from one form to another and he gained his power by always drinking from a certain pool.

Buffalo often travelled across a high mountain. One day, he said to the mountain, "Would you like to be changed into something else?"

"I would like to be something that nobody climbed over," said the mountain.

Buffalo used his spirit power to change the mountain into a very large stone. "Now you are hard so that no one can break you," he said, "and smooth so that you cannot be climbed. And I give you the power to change into anything else, as long as you don't break yourself."

On the other side of the mountains lived men who hunted animals. Buffalo decided to visit them and try to persuade them to change their ways.

Buffalo crossed the mountains to the other side. He came to a lodge, where he was greeted by an old woman and her grandson, who made him welcome.

"I have the power to change you into anything you choose," said Buffalo. "What would you like to be?"

"I want only to be with my grandson," said the old woman. "Wherever he goes, I wish to be."

"Then come home with me," said Buffalo. "We will teach the boy to be a swift runner and wherever he goes, you shall be."

So the grandmother and the boy followed Buffalo over the mountains to the other side.

The other buffaloes promised to teach the boy to run swiftly, if he agreed to teach his people

44

when he got older not to hunt them.

Then, Buffalo drank from the pool and used his spirit power to change the grandmother into Wind, so that wherever the boy went, she would be.

The boy stayed with the buffaloes until he was a man. Then the buffaloes reminded him of his promise and he returned to live with his people.

As he was such a swift runner he soon became the leader of the hunters and he was given the name Eagle Wing.

One day, the chief asked Eagle Wing to lead the other hunters over the mountains and bring back the meat and hide of the buffaloes for the tribe.

"If you do this for our people you will become chief one day," he said.

Eagle Wing was ambitious and wanted to be chief of his people, so, forgetting his promise, he agreed.

He led the hunters over the mountains, but ran so swiftly that he was soon far ahead. When he reached the land of the buffaloes he hunted them without mercy.

The great Buffalo was away roaming the valleys when this happened. On his journey home, he was struck with thirst and as he was too far from his special pool, he drank from another. When he saw what Eagle Wing had done he was very angry. He tried to turn the hunters into grass, but because he had drunk from another pool his spirit power was gone.

Buffalo went to the stone that was once a mountain. "Help me punish the hunter for what he has done," he asked.

Then Stone bent and tangled the straight trees and bushes, so that men could never again find an easy path, and broke himself into many pieces, so that men hurt their feet on the scattered stones. This punishment Eagle Wing brought upon his people, for not keeping his promise to the buffalo.

NORTH AMERICA

NORTH AMERICA

PRAIRIE WOLF

In the beginning, the Karuk people who lived on the shores of the Klamath River had everything they needed – except fire. Nights were long and cold in their country, but the only fire in the world was guarded by two old sisters, who lived beside the mouth of the river.

The Karuk tried to persuade the old sisters to share their fire and some tried to steal it, but without success.

At last, they decided to ask cunning Prairie Wolf for help.

The Karuk travelled to the desert to find Prairie Wolf. They presented him with fine buffalo steaks, for they knew he was always hungry, and offered him friendship in return for his help.

Cunning Prairie Wolf saw that helping the Karuk would be an easier way to fill his belly than hunting all day, so he agreed to fetch the fire.

That night, Prairie Wolf made a plan. The next morning, he asked Frog to wait near the Karuk's camp and Squirrel, Bat, Bear and Cougar to wait further along the track.

Lastly, he instructed one of the Karuk to hide close to the hut where the old sisters lived.

Then Prairie Wolf hung his head and scratched at the door of the hut. One of the sisters opened the door. Behind her, Prairie Wolf saw the bright fire blazing. Pretending to be weary and cold, he staggered inside and dropped to the floor with a shiver.

The old sisters weren't afraid of Prairie Wolf.

"Come near the fire," they said, so Prairie Wolf settled himself near the fire. Then, when they weren't looking, he edged a little closer and a little closer.

As soon as he was within a paw's reach of the flames, he barked a signal to the Karuk hunter who was hiding in the bushes nearby.

When the hunter heard the signal he began to hurl stones at the hut.

The angry sisters hurried outside to see who had dared to cause them trouble.

At once, Prairie Wolf seized a burning stick from the fire, and rushed out of the hut and down the track.

The old sisters saw the flame dance away through the trees and realised they'd been tricked. They chased after Prairie Wolf, shrieking with fury.

Prairie Wolf ran like the wind, but the old sisters followed at such a pace that they were soon close behind.

As they stretched out their bony hands to grasp his tail, Prairie Wolf flung the burning stick to Cougar, who caught it and ran on.

Cougar leapt along the track until he saw Bear ahead of him and handed him the burning stick.

Bear then carried the burning stick on until Bat swooped down to take her turn.

Bat tried to lose the old sisters in the wood, but still they followed. When she could fly no longer, Bat dropped the stick for Squirrel, who scampered along the track to where Frog was waiting. By this time, the stick was almost burned away.

At last, Frog reached a lake close to the Karuk village. He swallowed the stump of fire stick and dived into the water.

When the two old sisters reached the water's edge they could only stand and shake their bony fists, for neither of them had ever learned to swim.

On the other side of the lake, the Karuk were waiting with kindling for the fire. Frog climbed out of the water and spat the last few sparks at the kindling, which blazed into life.

At last, the Karuk could roast their meat and sleep warmly. They rewarded Prairie Wolf with plenty of good food so that he never needed to hunt again.

However, it wasn't long before the Karuk asked Prairie Wolf to help them once more.

The two old sisters had the key to a great dam, which was keeping all the salmon from swimming upstream. "Will you open the dam for us, Prairie Wolf, and let the shining salmon swim free?" they asked.

Prairie Wolf agreed to try to help, but decided to wait until his winter coat had changed colour.

When spring came, the two sisters didn't recognise the well fed Prairie Wolf who knocked on their door. They welcomed him and let him rest in their hut.

The next morning, one of the sisters took the key of the dam from the cupboard so that she could fetch a salmon for breakfast. Prairie Wolf stood up, stretched and followed her idly outside.

NORTH AMERICA

Once the sister had set off along the path, he ran ahead and flung himself between her feet, so that she tripped and let the key fly out of her hand.

Prairie Wolf seized the key, hurried to the dam and unlocked it.

Then the shining salmon escaped into the river in such numbers that the water seemed alive with fish. They swam away upstream, where the Karuk were waiting.

From that day forward, the Karuk caught all the salmon they wanted.

They were thankful and showed Prairie Wolf great honour.

However, Prairie Wolf grew very proud of his adventures and wasn't satisfied with their friendship.

He became so pleased with himself that he wanted to dance with the stars.

Night after night he howled at the sky, until a blue star took pity on him.

She called down to him and told him to stand on the high cliff, and there she reached down to him with her hand.

Prairie Wolf took the star's hand and together they danced through the night sky. But as she lifted him higher he began to grow cold.

Still he danced on, going higher and higher, and getting colder and colder, until his paws were numb. Suddenly, he slipped from the star's hand…

With a howl, proud, cunning Prairie Wolf fell down into the great chasm between the sky and the earth at the edge of the world and he was never seen again.

NORTH AMERICA

THE MERMAID OF THE MAGDALENES

Far off the coast of Canada are a group of lonely, rugged islands called the Magdalenes. Many fishermen used to sail there and risk the wild waves and rocks to catch tiny sardines, which they packed into boxes and sold onshore. The traders who bought them became wealthy by selling the sardines all around the world.

There was nothing the sardines could do to escape the fishing nets and their numbers grew smaller and smaller. In despair, they went to Lobster, who was the most powerful creature in the undersea kingdom, and asked for his help.

Lobster called a meeting of all the creatures of the sea, who came from the rock pools and the open water and the deep, dark ocean bed.

"The sardines are in danger," he told them. "Men are catching so many of them that soon they will all be gone."

"What can we do to help?" asked the skate.

"We must punish anyone who eats or fishes for a sardine," said Lobster. The creatures of the sea agreed. They all took an oath to punish anyone who ate or fished for their tiny cousins.

A short while later, a ship packed with boxes of sardines was wrecked on the rocks of the Magdalene Islands. The wild waves smashed up the wreckage and flung it onto the shore.

That evening, when the water was calm, a young girl whose father was a trader, took a walk along the beach. To her delight she found a box of sardines. The young girl loved the taste of the little fish more than anything and so she decided to eat them. However, try as she might, she couldn't open the box. With a sigh, she sat on a rock and sang to herself.

"I love sardines when they're boiled with beans
And mixed with the sands of the sea."

Nearby, the skate heard her singing and swam up close to the shore. When he heard the words of her song he remembered his oath to the sardines, but he was too shy to punish the girl, so he swam away.

Beyond the rocks, a merman also heard the song. He wanted a wife from the land to live with him in the sea, so he dressed in a suit of seaweed and hurried to the shore.

When he heard the words of the song he, too, remembered the oath he had made to the sardines. But with one glance, the merman had fallen in love with the young girl and couldn't bear to punish her, so he, too, swam away.

The moon came up and the girl grew hungry. She knocked the box against a rock, hoping to break it open, without success. Unknown to her, she woke Lobster, who had been fast asleep under the rock. When the girl began to sing again he listened to her words.

"I love sardines when they're boiled with beans
And mixed with the sands of the sea."

Lobster came out of his hiding place. "Let me help you open that box," he said gently.

The young girl thanked him and knelt down at the water's edge. But as soon as she held the box out to him, Lobster grasped her hand with his strong claw and swam away with her far out to sea.

Nobody knew what happened to the young trader's daughter, but some say she married a merman. She often sings, trying to lure islanders onto the rocks to keep her company. On those nights, the fishermen stay ashore, leaving the tiny sardines to swim safe from harm.

NORTH AMERICA

NORTH AMERICA
A NATIVE AMERICAN INDIAN STORY

WHY THE SWALLOW'S TAIL IS FORKED

In the beginning, the Great Spirit made all the animals content but, before long, he was disappointed to hear them complaining to each other, so he asked them to come to his lodge. The first to arrive were the creatures that could fly, then the creatures that walked and lastly the creatures that slithered and crawled.

"I have heard you complaining to each other," said the Great Spirit. "Tell me your troubles and I will do what I can to help."

Bear stood up. "I don't like to hunt for so long for my food," he said.

Then Bluebird spoke, "I don't like building a nest."

"I don't like living in a tree," said Squirrel and, one by one, all the animals came forward with their complaints. The last one to speak was Man.

"And what troubles you?" asked the Great Spirit.

"Snake likes to feast on my blood," said Man. "Can you give him some other food?"

"Why should I do that?" asked the Great Spirit.

"Because I am the first of all the creatures you made," said Man.

"That is true," agreed the Great Spirit, "you are the first, but I am father to them all. Snake has a right to his food. But maybe there is something I can do." The Great Spirit gazed upon all his creatures. "Mosquito," he said, "you travel far and wide. Fly among my creatures and find out who has the best blood for the snake. We shall all meet again to hear your judgement in a year and a day."

The animals went away to their homes in the rivers and the mountains, the forests and the prairies, to wait for the mosquito to do what the Great Spirit had commanded. For a year and a day, he travelled around the world tasting every creature, to find out whose blood would be best for Snake.

NORTH AMERICA

When it was time to gather once more at the lodge of the Great Spirit, all the animals came from the rivers and the mountains, the forests and the prairies. On the way, Mosquito looked up and saw Swallow.

"Good day," he said.

"Good day," said Swallow. "Have you discovered whose blood is best for Snake?"

"Oh yes," said Mosquito, "I have tasted every animal's blood and there is no doubt that it is the blood of Man."

Swallow was Man's friend, but she knew that Mosquito didn't like him.

"How can I prevent Mosquito from delivering his judgement?" she wondered. Then she had an idea.

She asked, once again, whose blood was best for Snake. This time, when Mosquito opened his mouth to answer, she pecked out his tiny tongue.

"Ksss-ksss-ksss!" buzzed Mosquito angrily and he flew away to the lodge of the Great Spirit.

When all the animals were gathered together once more, the Great Spirit turned to Mosquito and asked whose blood was best for Snake, but Mosquito could only buzz. "Ksss-ksss-ksss!"

Everyone was puzzled.

"Great Father," said Swallow, "Mosquito is shy and cannot answer you. When I met him on his way here, he told me that Frog's blood was best for Snake. Isn't that so, friend Mosquito?"

Mosquito darted about in a temper, but all he could say was "Ksss-ksss-ksss!"

"So, Snake shall eat Frog's blood," said the Great Spirit, "and Man will no longer be troubled by Snake."

Then Snake was angry with Swallow, for he didn't like the taste of Frog's blood.

As Swallow flew past, he seized her by the tail and tore a little piece away.

That is the reason why the swallow's tail is forked and why Man always thinks of her as a friend.

RABBIT AND THE MOON MAN

It was midwinter. Deep snow lay everywhere and Rabbit and his grandmother were hungry.

Rabbit had set traps around the forest to catch something to eat, but for several days his traps had been empty. When he went to inspect them he found plenty of animal and bird tracks in the snow, but nothing for him to take home for dinner.

"I think somebody is stealing from my traps," said Rabbit.

"Then you must go out earlier and get to them before the thief," said his grandmother. But no matter how early Rabbit went out, he always returned empty handed.

He would tiptoe silently, moving like a shadow from tree to tree as he approached his traps, in the hope of catching the culprit. But no matter what he tried, the thief would always evade him.

Then, one morning, after a fresh fall of snow, Rabbit noticed an unusual footprint beside one of his traps; it was long and thin and as light and delicate as a moonbeam.

That night, Rabbit made a snare from a strong bowstring and laid it beside the trap. Then, holding the other end of the bowstring, he hid from sight behind a clump of trees and waited.

"At last I shall see who has been stealing my dinner," he thought to himself. "When the thief comes along and steps into the snare, I shall pull it tight and tie him to a tree!"

Rabbit sat silently watching the snow sparkle in the moonlight as he waited for the thief to arrive. Suddenly, the Moon disappeared and only the stars were left to light the night sky.

Rabbit felt nervous in the dark. Suddenly, he heard the sound of someone moving through the trees. A white light appeared, dazzling Rabbit's eyes. It moved slowly towards the trap and stopped exactly where Rabbit had laid his snare.

"Now I've got you!" cried Rabbit.

He pulled the bowstring tight and quickly tied the other end to a tree. There was the sound of a struggle, but the white light stayed fixed to the spot.

Rabbit was afraid of the dazzling light, but he bravely crept closer to take a look at the man of the long-foot.

However, staring into the brightness made his eyes sore, so Rabbit bathed them in a nearby stream.

But that didn't help, and only made him cross. He threw snowballs at the light to try to put it out, but the snowballs just melted away. Then he took fistfuls of mud from the stream and hurled them at the shining light.

"Ouch!" cried a voice. "You've splattered my face with mud! Come and untie me at once. I am the Man in the Moon and I must get away before sunrise."

Rabbit was frightened. He ran home to tell his grandmother. "Oh dear," she cried, "you must untie him or there will be trouble!"

Rabbit returned to the Man in the Moon but kept his distance. "I will free you," he said, "if you promise never to come to earth and steal from my traps again."

"I swear by my light," promised the Man in the Moon. Then Rabbit shut his eyes and crept forward, feeling his way.

His lip quivered at the great heat of the Moon and his shoulders were scorched, but just as the first light of dawn glowed through the trees, Rabbit edged close enough to gnaw through the bowstring with his teeth and release his prisoner.

The Moon jumped into the sky at once and has kept his promise to stay there ever since.

Sometimes he goes away to try to wash off the marks of the mud Rabbit threw at him, and then the sky is dark. But on a moonlit night, you can still clearly see from the splats on his face, that he never succeeds.

Sadly, since their encounter with the Man in the Moon, rabbits have never been quite the same either.

To this day, they have never managed to soothe their pink eyelids, which are still sore from staring into the bright light. Their lips still quiver from the fear of approaching such a scorching heat, and their shoulders remain a burnt yellow, even when they are wearing their white winter coats.

NORTH AMERICA

WHY THE BEAR HAS A STUMPY TAIL

NORTH AMERICA

One winter's day, Bear met Fox, who was carrying a string of fish. Bear gazed at the fish with hungry eyes.

"That's a good dinner you've got there," he said. "How did you catch so many?"

"It's easy if you know the secret," said sly Fox. "Someone with a fine tail like you could catch himself plenty of fish."

Bear licked his lips at the thought of it. "What's the secret?" he asked.

Fox looked over his shoulder to check that no one else was listening, as if he was going to share a big secret.

Then he whispered to Bear, "Go out onto the frozen lake and cut a hole in the ice. Then stick your tail through the hole into the water and wait for the fish to bite." Bear listened carefully.

"The fish won't be able to resist your fine, fat tail," said Fox. "It may hurt a little when they bite, but be patient — the longer you can wait, the more tasty fish you'll catch."

"When you think you've got enough, just pull your tail out with a quick, strong tug," continued Fox with a smile.

Bear thanked Fox warmly and hurried down to the lake, eager to catch himself a good dinner. He licked his lips hungrily at the thought of all the fish he would catch.

He cut a hole in the ice and sat with his tail dangling in the water. The cold soon made his tail hurt. "Aha!" he thought. "The fish are starting to bite!" All afternoon he sat, imagining the delicious fish he was catching. At last, he couldn't wait any longer.

But when Bear tried to stand up he couldn't move. "These fish are heavy," he thought with a smile. Then he remembered that Fox told him to pull his tail out with a quick, strong tug.

Bear tugged hard and up he stood — but not one fish came out of the ice hole, and not much tail either, for it was stuck fast in the frozen lake!

Since that day, bears have always had stumpy tails and have never trusted a fox.

NORTH AMERICA
AN INUIT STORY

THE BLIND BOY AND THE LOON

Long ago, in a land of snow and ice, a woman lived with her daughter and son in an igloo. The boy was skilled at hunting with a bow and harpoon and always returned from a hunting trip with plenty of game on his sled. This he gave to his mother, who cleaned and skinned the animals and prepared the meat. Thanks to the boy's love of hunting, the storage platforms around their igloo were always well packed with food and the family were never hungry.

The girl was grateful for everything her brother caught, but their mother was lazy and complained about all the tasks she had to do. "Your brother causes me work, work, work without rest," she moaned. As time went by, the woman began to hate her son's hunting trips.

One day, while he was sleeping, she cut a small piece of blubber and rubbed it onto his eyes. As she did so, she wished that he would become blind.

When the boy woke the next morning, his eyesight was gone.

The boy's sister comforted him, but being blind meant he was no longer able to hunt and could do nothing but sit on his bed all day. Then his mother scorned him for his uselessness. When their food ran out, she trapped foxes and squirrels to eat, but only gave the boy scraps in his bowl and dirty water to drink.

The family lived this way for many months until, one winter's day, a huge polar bear came to the igloo and began beating at the thin ice window. The boy felt blindly for his bow, took aim and shot an arrow towards the bear, killing it at once.

"Fool!" cried his mother. "You just frightened it away." But soon the boy smelled bear-meat cooking and knew that she had lied. His mother kept the good meat and handed him a bowl of old fox stew. The boy said nothing, but as soon as his mother went out to fetch water, his sister gave him her own supper.

Four years passed. The woman treated her son no better than a dog and it was only thanks

57

to his sister's kindness that he kept strong.

Then, one night, while his mother and sister slept, the blind boy heard the haunting cry of a loon. Knowing that the bird would be on the lake, he crawled out of the igloo on his hands and knees and followed the bird's voice down to the water's edge. There he sat and imagined the moonlit view.

To his surprise, the loon spoke. "Your mother made you blind while you slept," she said. "Let me carry you down into the water of the lake, for it will wash away your blindness."

"How can that be?" asked the boy in wonder.

"Trust me," said the loon. "Lie on my back and take a deep breath. When you can hold your breath no longer, lay your head against my neck."

The boy was sure that the loon was too small to carry him, but as he reached out to climb onto her back he felt her grow as large as a kayak. He took a deep breath and she dived into the water of the lake.

Down, down, down she dived and the boy held tight as the cold water streamed across his face. When he could hold his breath no longer, the boy laid his head against her neck, and she returned to the surface.

"Now, what can you see?" asked the loon.

The boy blinked and stared. "A pale light," he said.

"Then we must dive again," said the loon.

When they came up for the second time she asked the boy what he could see.

"Everything!" he said in amazement. "I can even see the tiniest rocks on the far mountain!"

"That is too much," said the loon, and she took him down into the water of the lake once again. When the boy emerged the third time, his eyesight was restored to its normal strength.

NORTH AMERICA

NORTH
AMERICA

"How can I thank you for your kindness?" he asked the loon.

"Just put some fish in the lake for me now and then," said the loon. "I need nothing else."

When the boy went home he was horrified to see that the skins his mother had made him sleep on were covered in lice and his bowl and cup were filthy, but he said nothing. He waited until his mother woke up and asked her for a drink. Moaning as usual, she filled his cup with dirty water and handed it to him.

"Throw that away and give me the fresh water you drink yourself!" said the boy.

His sister gasped with joy. "You can see!" she cried. His mother pretended to be pleased but there was anger in her eyes.

It took many days for the boy to regain his strength after sitting in the igloo for so long, but as soon as spring came and the ice melted, he was eager to go hunting once more. "Come with me, Mother," he said, "and we shall catch a whale."

His mother was very fond of whale meat, so she followed her son down to the shore and they took his old whale boat out to sea. They soon saw many small whales, but the boy paddled on until a big whale swam close to the boat.

Working quickly, he took aim and threw his harpoon so that it caught fast in the whale's back, and then he slung the other end of the harpoon line around his mother's wrist and pulled it tight. With a scream she tried to free herself, but the whale tugged her over the side of the boat and away through the water.

Some said the woman became a narwhal when she disappeared beneath the waves that day. Some say they can still hear her cruel voice on the icy wind.

NORTH AMERICA
A NATIVE AMERICAN INDIAN STORY

THE FIRST WOODPECKER

In times past, the Great Spirit would come down from the sky and walk among his people on earth, in the form of an old man.

Once, as he walked through the forest, he came across a woman sitting outside her wigwam. "I have fasted for many days," he said. "Will you give me some food?"

"Come into my wigwam," said the woman. "If you wait, I will make you a cake."

"I will wait," said the Great Spirit.

Then the woman made a very small cake and put it to bake on the fire. When it was cooked she was surprised, for it seemed larger than before. "I'm not going to give an old man a good cake like that," she thought. She put it away for herself and asked him to wait while she made another one.

"I will wait," said the Great Spirit.

To her astonishment, when the second cake was baked it was larger than the first. "This is fine enough for a feast," she thought.

"That cake was not good enough," she told the Great Spirit. "If you wait a little longer I will make another one."

"I will wait," said the Great Spirit.

Then the woman made another cake. This time she made it much smaller than the others, but when it was cooked it was the biggest of all, as the Great Spirit had worked his power upon the cake.

"This will feed me for many days," she thought. So she hid the cake under a blanket and told her guest that she had nothing for him after all. "Go and find yourself food in the forest," she said. "There are plenty of insects to eat in the bark of the trees."

The Great Spirit was angry. He stood up and threw back his cloak. "A woman should be kind and good-hearted, but you are selfish and cruel," he said. "Therefore, you shall live in the forest from now on and find insects to eat in the bark of the trees."

Then the Great Spirit stamped his foot and the woman began to shrink. Feathers grew all over her body, her arms became wings, and she became the first woodpecker.

THE BADGER AND THE BEAR

Old Father Badger was a great hunter. He had many children who were always well fed and their underground home on the edge of the forest had a good store of meat, which Mother Badger sliced and dried and packed into painted bags.

One day, Father Badger stayed at home to make new arrows and his children gathered around to watch and learn. Suddenly, they heard a noise outside the door. A huge shaggy bear pushed open the door flap and peered inside, sniffing the scent of food. The young badgers were frightened of the stranger's gruff voice and long claws, but their father invited him inside.

"You look hungry, friend," said Father Badger. "Will you share our meal?"

"Yes, I'm starving," said the bear. "Give me meat to eat, my friend." And he sat down by the door with crossed shins.

Mother Badger cooked up her best venison and gave the bear all he could eat and when he was full he smacked his lips with satisfaction and returned to the forest.

After that, the bear came most days to be fed, always sitting by the door with crossed shins. Mother Badger put a fur rug in his place so that their guest was comfortable.

As weeks passed, the bear grew strong with Mother Badger's good cooking. One day he arrived with a wicked gleam in his eye. Instead of sitting in his usual place he stood tall on the rug.

"Welcome, friend," said Father Badger. "Will you share our meal?"

The bear raised his paw. "See how strong I am now?" he said with a menacing smile. At the sight of his sharp teeth the little badgers hid behind their mother in fear.

"I have no home, no bags of dried meat or arrows," said the bear. "You must give me yours!"

"We have shared our food and friendship," said Father Badger. "Please don't take our home!"

But the bear stepped forward and growled fiercely. Mother Badger gathered her children and hurried them out of the house.

"This is my home now!" roared the bear. "Be gone or I'll throw you out." Father Badger took one last look at his home, his bags of dried meat and his arrows and hurried out of the door.

The Badger family fled into the forest.

"Don't worry, my children," said Father Badger, "I will build us somewhere to sleep tonight." When they came to a clearing, he built a small hut out of bent willows and covered it with dry grass and twigs. But, without his arrows, Father Badger couldn't hunt for food. The sound of his children crying with hunger hurt him like a poisoned arrow wound.

"I shall go begging for food," he told to his wife next morning. Then he disguised himself in a long robe and went back to their old home.

The bear had fetched his cubs to join him and sat outside, slicing meat to dry while they played in the sunshine.

"I am starving, friend," said Father Badger. "Will you give me meat to eat?"

The bear snarled angrily. "Be gone," he growled, shaking his paw, "or I'll kick you out!"

With a heavy heart Father Badger turned to go, but he tripped over a big root and fell to the ground. All the bear cubs laughed except the youngest, who was not unkind because he was used to being laughed at himself. The youngest bear cub followed Father Badger back to his willow hut. When he saw the little badgers crying with hunger he felt sorry for them, so that evening, he slipped away from home and left a small piece of meat outside the badgers' hut.

The next day, Father Badger went back to the bear and begged for food again, but the bear just roared angrily and pushed him to the ground. However, beside the place where Father Badger fell, there was a leaf red with blood that had dripped from a piece of buffalo meat, so he waited until the bear turned away, hid it under his robe and took it back to his family.

Father Badger showed the buffalo blood to his wife. "I shall pray to the Great Spirit to bless this," he said. First he built a small lodge, where he performed a sacred ceremony; sprinkling water upon hot stones to purify himself and the buffalo blood. Then he asked the Great Spirit for a blessing. After sitting in silence for a while, Father Badger stepped out of the lodge. To his surprise, a fine young brave carrying a magic arrow followed him.

"My son!" exclaimed Father Badger, admiring the brave's buckskin trousers and long fringed quiver. "You have sprung from the blood of the buffalo to answer my prayer."

"Yes, Father," said the young brave. "I am here to help you."

Then Father Badger told the young brave how his kindness to the bear had been repaid with cruelty. "My children are starving and, without arrows, I can only beg the bear for food."

"Then tomorrow I shall go with you," said the young brave.

The next day, as the bear was taking some slices of meat off the drying poles, he saw Father Badger come out of the forest. Before he could raise his paws in anger, the young brave stepped forward, carrying his magic arrow. Bear had heard about the coming of a man with a magic arrow long ago and was afraid. "Friend," he said, "take my knife and cut yourself some meat."

"This is my father's knife," said the young brave. "You must return all that belongs to him."

Bear cowered with fear. He dropped to his feet, called his cubs and ran away to the forest.

"Now justice has been done," said the young brave and the grateful badgers thanked him warmly and returned to their home.

NORTH AMERICA

HOW THE KING OF THE BIRDS WAS CHOSEN

There was a time, long ago, when the birds of the Mayan land often quarrelled with one another. Their noisy arguments disturbed the Great Spirit, who wanted peace among his creatures, so he called a meeting in the forest and told the birds to choose themselves a king, to settle their disputes.

Many birds wanted to be king. The cardinal bird strutted before the others, displaying his brilliant red feathers. "Look at my beautiful crest," he boasted, "it looks just like a crown. I should be king!"

But the mockingbird laughed at him. "A king must have a fine voice so that his subjects pay attention to him," he said and he performed a beautiful melody. "Everyone listens to me when I sing, so I should be king."

"No, no, no," gobbled the wild turkey. "What use is a pretty voice? A king must be powerful so that he can protect his subjects. I'm the biggest, strongest bird of us all, so it

should be me who becomes your king."

One bird after another put himself forward and showed off his talents, but none seemed to have all the right qualities. Nobody could agree on who would make the best king.

Meanwhile, Quetzal watched from the back of the crowd. He was clever and ambitious, but he knew that his drab feathers wouldn't impress the others. He slipped away and went to find his friend Roadrunner, who was busy with his job as a messenger of the roads.

"Roadrunner, my friend," said Quetzal, "there is no one to rival the beauty of your handsome feathers, but I know you are too humble to put yourself forward as king of the Birds. However, I am very suitable for the job, with my superior intelligence and great wisdom, but I lack a magnificent coat to wear when I present myself before the other birds."

Shy Roadrunner fluttered his emerald-green wings and swished his long, shimmering tail.

Quetzal hopped a little closer. "Sadly, I cannot lend you my brilliant mind," he said, "but you could lend me your feathers awhile, just to impress the other birds."

Roadrunner wasn't keen to part with his stunning feathers, but Quetzal worked hard to persuade him of his good intentions and friendship. "When I am king I will repay you with great riches and honours," he promised. At last Roadrunner agreed that Quetzal would make a good king and should be given a chance. As soon as he did so, the feathers began to disappear from his body and grow upon Quetzal.

Proud Quetzal admired his new jewel-like coat and elegant tail. Raising his golden beak with a royal air, he went to present himself before the other birds. "You all know that I am clever and wise," said Quetzal, "but a king must also be magnificent and there is no other bird in the forest as magnificent as me!" Then all the birds agreed that Quetzal was the most impressive and the Great Spirit was pleased and declared that he should be their king.

But once he was crowned, Quetzal was kept busy settling quarrels and keeping the peace among his fellow birds and he quite forgot about returning the feathers he had borrowed.

Some of the birds noticed that Roadrunner had not been seen since the day of the king-making and organised a search for him. They soon found him hiding, cold and hungry, without a feather on his body. When they heard what had happened, each bird gave Roadrunner some feathers of their own. Today, Roadrunner still wears a strange suit of many different feathers and calls 'Puhuy?', which means 'Where is he?'

NORTH AMERICA

THE BEAR PRINCE

Once upon a time there was a poor woodcutter who had three daughters.

One day, while he was working in the forest, a huge bear appeared and grabbed the axe from his hands.

"How dare you chop down the trees in my forest," roared the bear. "I have a mind to chop you down instead!"

The woodcutter fell to his knees, trembling. "Please forgive me," he said. "I only take wood to sell so that I can buy food for my three daughters. If you chop me down they will starve."

The bear looked at the axe thoughtfully. "I will spare your life if one of your daughters will be my wife," he said. "Then you may take all the wood you need."

The woodcutter was horrified at this request, but to refuse would leave all his daughters to starve, so reluctantly he agreed to the bear's demand.

The bear returned the axe and the woodcutter hurried home. When he explained what had happened, his two eldest daughters turned pale. "Marry a bear? Never!" they cried. "We would rather starve, Father!"

But the youngest daughter, Ninfa, saw the despair in her father's eyes.

"I will keep your promise, Father," she said.

So, the following day, with a heavy heart, the woodcutter fetched the priest and took Ninfa into the woods to marry the bear.

Once they were married, the bear led Ninfa to his cave. He brought her a chest of beautiful clothes and left her until sunset. When it was dark he returned and chanted: *"Bear so hairy, Bear so alarming, change into a prince, handsome and charming."*

In an instant, the bear became a handsome prince. "Don't be afraid, Ninfa," he said. "I've been cursed by a witch to live like a bear and only return to my true form at night. You have shown such bravery.

Can you keep my secret?"

Ninfa promised to keep her husband's secret. The next morning, at sunrise, the prince said:

"Prince so handsome, prince so charming, change into a bear, so hairy and alarming."

And he became the bear once more.

Ninfa was happy with her Bear Prince, but as time passed she missed her family and asked if she could visit them. The Bear Prince agreed and reminded her not to reveal his secret.

Ninfa's father greeted her with great joy, but her sisters saw the beautiful clothes and were jealous. They taunted her for marrying a bear. "What a waste of fine silk when nobody will see you but a hairy brute!" they said. At first, Ninfa took no notice, but they kept repeating their unkind words until she lost her temper and told them the prince's secret.

Her sisters were amazed. "You must break the curse!" they told Ninfa. "Wait until the prince is asleep, then tie a scarf around his mouth so that he cannot say the magic words. You'll save him from being a bear forever."

When Ninfa returned to the Bear Prince she did just as her sisters had told her. "He will surely be pleased," she thought.

The prince woke at sunrise to find that he couldn't repeat the magic words and so the curse was ended, but to Ninfa's dismay her husband looked broken-hearted.

"You forgot your promise," he said sadly. "To undo the spell we had to live as man and wife for a year and a day. Now I must leave and you must search for me until you find the Castle of Faith." And with those words he vanished.

Ninfa felt desperately unhappy, for she had grown to love the prince. But she knew that her tears wouldn't unite them again, so she set off to find the Castle of Faith.

Ninfa hadn't travelled far when she met a wizard and asked him the way to the Castle of Faith. The wizard hadn't heard of it, but he told her to walk on to his father's house and ask there.

"Take this nut," the wizard said. "If you are ever in trouble, break it open."

The young girl thanked him and continued on to the house of the wizard's father, where she asked him the same question, but he knew nothing about the Castle of Faith. "Go to my brother's house and ask him," he said and he gave her another nut. "If you ever find yourself in trouble, break this open."

The third wizard didn't know where to find the Castle of Faith either, but he suggested that she ask the Moon. Like his brother, he gave Ninfa a nut and told her to break it open if she were ever in trouble.

Ninfa thanked the wizard and walked on to the house of the Moon. It was night by the time she reached it. The Moon was so cold she made Ninfa shiver. "I cannot help

NORTH AMERICA

you," she said, "but the Sun may know how to find the Castle of Faith."

Although she was weary, Ninfa went on, still believing she could find the prince. When she came to the Sun's house it was so hot that she had to hide behind the fence. "I know the castle you seek," said the Sun, "but I cannot go out after dark. I will call for my friend the Wind to take you there."

To Ninfa's delight, the Wind came and swept her up in his arms. With hope in her heart she flew across the land until he set her gently down beside a castle, where a fiesta was taking place. "Good luck!" whistled the Wind and he rushed away.

Ninfa crept quietly into the ballroom, but what she saw made her heart turn to stone. There sat the prince with a new bride, eating a wedding feast. She didn't know that the bride was a witch who had blinded the prince with magic and tricked him into the

marriage. Suddenly the witch saw Ninfa. She screamed at the servants to throw her out, which caught the prince's attention.

The prince recognised Ninfa at once, but before he could speak, the witch's servants were upon her.

Ninfa remembered the nuts she'd been given by the wizards. She broke one and instantly became a little rat.

When the witch saw this she turned into a cat and chased her. Ninfa sprang onto the prince's plate and broke the second nut, which turned her into a grain of rice. She hid herself among the other grains on his plate, but the witch turned into a chicken and began to peck at the rice.

Then Ninfa broke the third nut, turned into a coyote and ate the chicken whole. At last she returned to her true form and was reunited with the prince, and from that moment they were never parted again.

NORTH AMERICA

COYOTE AND THE TURTLE

In a deep, cool river, where alligators lazed all day, there lived an inquisitive young turtle. She loved to swim from one bank to the other and explore the rocks and stones on the riverbed, but no matter what she found, she was always curious to see more.

One day, Turtle decided to explore the world beyond the river, so she crawled out of the water and took a walk into the desert. Turtle wandered among the spiky cactus plants, discovering snakes and scorpions and spiders and many other creatures she'd never seen before. She walked on and on, amazed at the wonders around her, not paying attention to how far she was straying from home.

The sun rose high over the desert and Turtle soon began to feel very hot. She longed for a drink and the feeling of cool water on her face. However, when she turned to go home she saw that the river was now far away.

"I'm so tired and thirsty, I'll never be able to walk that far," she sighed with dismay. So she crawled into the shade of a cactus plant. Looking out at the strange desert world, Turtle suddenly felt so far away from home that she began to cry.

She didn't notice Coyote nearby. "That's a lovely song the Turtle is singing," thought Coyote. "I'll ask her to teach it to me."

He trotted up to Turtle, crouched in the shadow of the cactus plant, and asked her to teach him her song.

"I'm not singing, Señor, I'm crying," sobbed Turtle.

Coyote thought he was being made a fool of. "I heard you with my own ears," he insisted. "If you don't teach me your song I'll eat you up right here for lunch!"

Turtle looked at Coyote's pink tongue and his sharp, pointed teeth and knew she must be clever to outwit him. She dried her tears. "I wouldn't be a good lunch for you," she said. "My shell is very hard and impossible to swallow."

Coyote looked at her shell and realised she was right. "Then I shall throw you out into the hot sunshine," he said.

"Oh, the hot sun doesn't bother me," said Turtle. "I've got very thick skin."

"So why are you hiding in the shade?" asked Coyote suspiciously.

"I'm not hiding, Señor," said Turtle, "I'm just listening to the cactus tell a sad story. That's why I was crying." Coyote stared at Turtle in disbelief, but he couldn't resist bending forward to hear for himself if it was true.

"Come closer," whispered Turtle. "The voice of the cactus is very quiet." Coyote bent closer and closer and...pricked his nose on a cactus spine!

"Ouch!" he yelled, crossly. "I shall throw you on the rocks, instead!"

"The rocks don't bother me," said Turtle. "I can pull my head and feet right inside my shell and just bounce away."

Coyote was determined to punish Turtle. "In that case," he said, "I shall throw you into the deep, cold river!"

Then Turtle pretended to be very afraid. "Oh no, Señor," she cried in a trembling voice, "please, not the river – I shall surely drown!"

"That will serve you right for making a fool of me," snapped Coyote, and he took Turtle in his mouth and flung her high over the cactus plants, over the snakes and scorpions and spiders, into the river with a splash.

Turtle plunged into the deep, cool water with delight. When she'd had a good, long drink she swam up to the surface. "Thank you for bringing me home, Señor!" she called happily and then Coyote realised just how cleverly he'd been tricked!

NORTH AMERICA

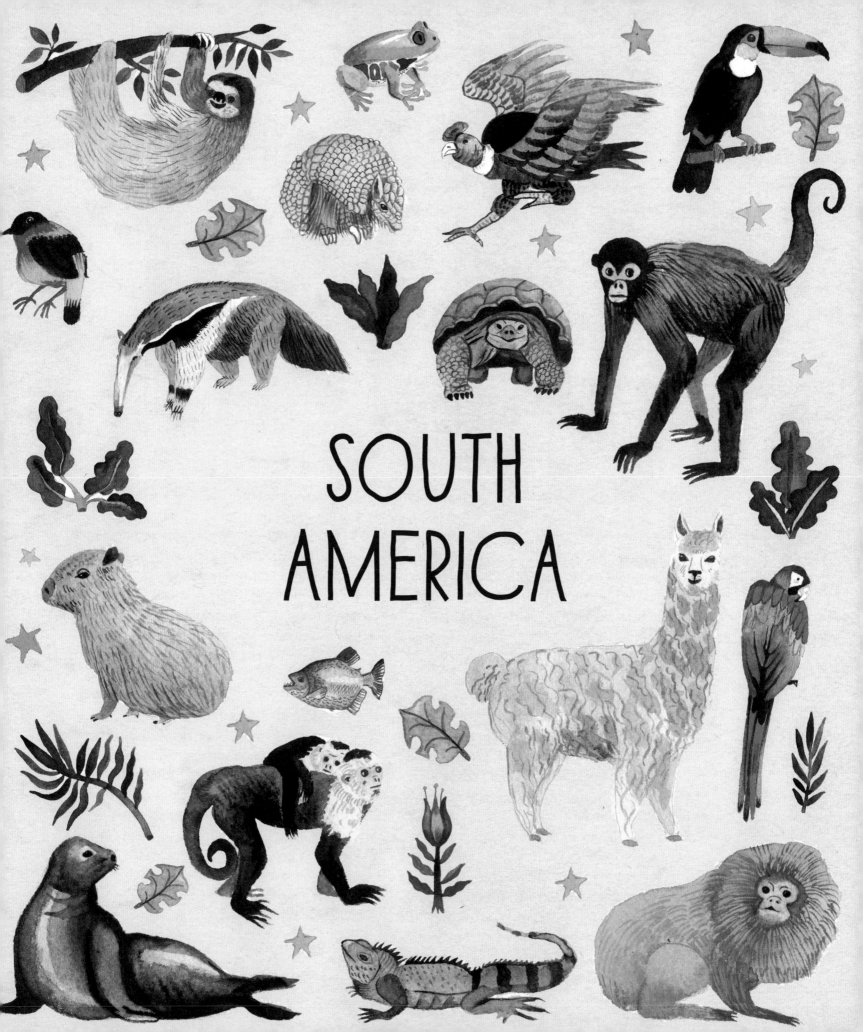

SOUTH
AMERICA

SOUTH AMERICA
A STORY FROM PERU

THE LITTLE FROG OF THE STREAM

There was once a frog who lived by a mountain stream. She could never bear to look at her reflection in the water, because she was born without the beautiful bright speckles that all her brothers and sisters had.

On a rocky ledge, high above the stream, lived a great condor. He had made himself a fine house there, with soft vicuña skins on the floor and a large feather bed.

One day, the condor noticed a young shepherdess tending to a herd of llamas in the meadow below. The shepherdess was called Collyur, which means "Morning Star".

"Now I have a fine house, I should have somebody to look after it," thought the condor. So, he flew down to the meadow, snatched Collyur up into the air and carried her home.

Collyur had no choice but to work hard for the condor, cleaning his house and preparing his meals. From the rocky ledge she could see her own home in the village far below, but she knew she could never escape the condor's sharp eyes.

Only the frog saw Collyur gazing sadly across the mountains. She wished that she could help the poor shepherdess.

One morning, Collyur asked the condor if she could go down to the stream to wash her clothes.

"No," said the condor. "You must stay here and cook for me."

"But the food is already cooked," said Collyur, "and all my duties are done."

The condor eyed her suspiciously. "How do I know you won't escape?" he asked.

Collyur thought fast. "You'll hear me beating the clothes on a rock to wash them," she said, "so you'll know where I am."

The condor reluctantly agreed to let Collyur go. "But don't be tempted to run away," he warned, "I shall be listening."

Collyur thanked the condor. She wrapped herself in a vicuña skin and made her clothes into a little bundle, then she climbed down from the rocky ledge and made her way to the stream. There, she washed her clothes and beat them on a rock, crying bitterly.

The little frog hopped up beside her. "Why are you so sad?" she asked.

Collyur dried her tears and gazed at the frog's kind face. "The condor captured me and I cannot escape," she sighed.

"Maybe I can help you," said the frog. "I have the power to change my form for a few moments. If I take on your appearance and beat those clothes on the rock, then you will have a chance to escape."

"Oh, thank you!" cried Collyur and she kissed the little frog on the forehead. As soon as Collyur put down the clothes, the frog took on her appearance and began beating them against the rock.

The condor finished eating his dinner, unaware that his housekeeper was running away down the mountain. "Where is that girl?" he grumbled. "Her clothes must be clean by now!" But when he stepped out onto the ledge to call her, the shepherdess appeared to plunge into the water and vanish right before his eyes!

The angry condor swooped down to the stream, but Collyur was nowhere to be found. Only the frog and the fishes knew what had happened.

When the frog went home to her brothers and sisters, they all stared at her in amazement. "Look at your reflection!" they cried. For Collyur's kiss on the frog's head had become a sparkling jewel, as beautiful as the morning star.

Then the fishes told the story of the frog's kindness, and from that day she was always proud to see her reflection in the mountain stream.

SOUTH
AMERICA

SOUTH AMERICA
A STORY FROM BOLIVIA

THE SONG OF THE ARMADILLO

Armadillo loved music more than anything else in the world. The sound of birds singing in the rain forest filled his heart with happiness and the rhythm of buzzing insects made his tiny feet want to dance.

When it rained, Armadillo loved to listen to the booming chorus of the frogs as they splashed in the forest pools. "I wish I could sing like you," he sighed.

But the frogs just laughed. "Don't be silly," they said. "Everyone knows that armadillos can't sing!"

Up in the trees, crickets were always chirruping a lively tune. "Can you teach me how to sing like you?" asked Armadillo.

But the crickets just giggled. "Don't be silly," they said. "Everyone knows armadillos can't sing!"

So Armadillo wandered through the forest, listening to the howling, squawking, twittering, drumming, warbling music of his fellow creatures, wishing with all his heart

that he could make music of his own.

One day, Armadillo came upon a man with a cage of canaries, resting by the side of the road. The canaries were singing with the sweetest voices Armadillo had ever heard. He crept up beside them to listen.

"Please teach me how to sing," he pleaded. "I love music more than anything else in the world — all I want is to be able to make music of my own."

The canaries flitted about the cage in amusement. "What a ridiculous wish!" they twittered. "Who ever heard of an armadillo making music?"

But the man overheard their conversation. "Don't listen to those silly birds, my friend," he said. "I understand your wish. I am a musician myself."

"Can you help me?" asked Armadillo.

The man studied the armadillo carefully. "Yes, I think I could help you to make beautiful music one day," he said, "but not yet. If you come to me when you are very, very old,

I promise I shall help you make music that will fill people's hearts with happiness. Until then, you must enjoy the music of others. Can you be content with that?"

"Oh yes," said Armadillo gratefully. "If I know I will make music one day then I can be happy." So he thanked the musician and returned to the songs of the rainforest.

Armadillo lived a long, happy life, but when he knew he was near the end of his days he went to find the musician, who greeted him like an old friend.

"Do you remember your promise?" asked Armadillo, gazing in wonder at all the instruments in the musician's house.

"Of course," said the musician. "Spend your last days here with me and I shall look after you. Then, when you die, I shall make a wonderful instrument from your shell,

which will play music that will fill many hearts with happiness."

Armadillo was overjoyed to think that his wish was finally going to come true. He spent his last happy days with the musician, who played and sang to him, until he finally fell into a deep sleep and died.

Then the musician made a charango from the armadillo's shell and strung it with ten strings. When it was finished, the charango made bright, beautiful music, full of life and the musician travelled throughout the land, playing in memory of his friend Armadillo.

When the frogs and crickets and canaries heard the sweet notes of the charango they listened in wonder. "At last Armadillo has a voice," they said. "Who would have guessed he would make the most beautiful music in the world!"

SOUTH AMERICA

SOUTH AMERICA
A STORY FROM ARGENTINA

THE TWO VISCACHAS

Two young viscachas lived together on the rocky slopes of the Andes Mountains. They were best friends and loved to play all day, chasing each other among the boulders and jumping from ledge to ledge.

The two friends shared everything, especially any delicious patch of moss or lichen, which was their favourite food. At night, when the air grew cold and a chilly wind blew through the mountains, they would find shelter in a crevice and huddle together to share their warmth as best they could.

One morning, the two viscachas noticed something red caught on a thorny bush. They scampered closer to take a look.

"It doesn't smell like anything to eat!" said one of them sadly.

His friend tugged at the bundle of red stuff. "It's a scrap of blanket," she said. "Maybe it was thrown away, or blown here by the wind." As she pulled it free from the thorns, the little scrap of red cloth ripped in two. The viscachas took a piece each.

"This is a real treasure!" said the first viscacha. "But what a pity it isn't the right size to cover me."

"This piece won't cover me, either," said his friend. "If only they were still joined together, we'd have a big enough blanket to keep us both warm at night."

As they sat, wondering what to do with their new-found treasure, Señor Fox came along. He eyed the two viscachas with a crafty smile.

"Hello, Amigos," he said. "What have you got there?"

"We found a treasure!" said the two viscachas. "It's a torn blanket. If only we could find a way to sew the pieces back together it would keep us both warm at night."

"Well, it's your lucky day!" said Señor Fox. "As it happens, I have a needle and thread.

I'd be happy to lend them to you, if you'll let me share your warm blanket on a cold night."

The two viscachas agreed that they must be very lucky and thanked Señor Fox for his offer, so he went to fetch a needle and thread from his den. When he returned, one of the viscachas sewed the two pieces of red blanket together. Senor Fox watched and waited. When the job was done, he took his needle, wished them both a good morning and went on his way.

The two viscachas laid their precious blanket on a rock and went off to play.

That evening, as the sun set, a chilly wind blew across the mountains. The two friends shivered in the cold night air, but they smiled to each other. "Tonight we'll have our warm blanket to sleep under," they said and they hurried back to where they had left it.

But, when they go there, sitting beside the red blanket was Señor Fox. "Good evening, amigos," he said. "I hope you remember your promise to share this warm blanket with me?"

"Yes, Señor," said the two viscachas, beginning to shudder with cold.

"Good," said Señor Fox. "It was my thread that stitched up the middle of the blanket so that part belongs to me." And he pulled the blanket right over himself, so that the two viscachas had to lie on either side, with hardly any blanket to cover them at all.

That night Señor Fox enjoyed a good, warm sleep, but the little shivering viscachas didn't sleep at all.

In the morning they crept away and left their treasure behind.

"It's better to trust a friend than make a bargain with Señor Fox!" they agreed.

SOUTH AMERICA

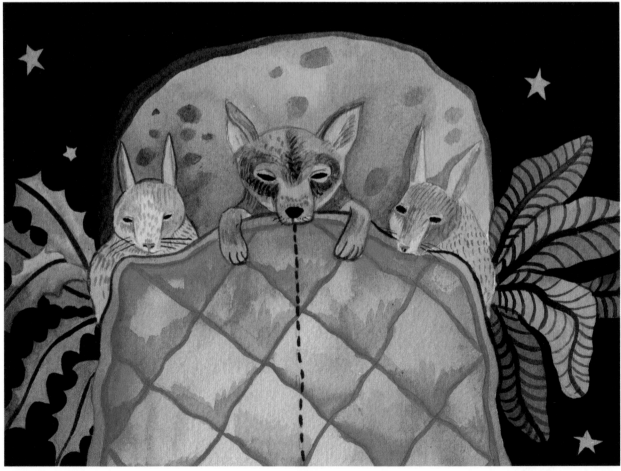

SOUTH AMERICA
A STORY
FROM BRAZIL

THE PARTY IN THE SKY

Toad didn't always look the way he does now, with lumps and bumps all over his body. There was a time when Toad had smooth skin and considered himself very handsome. In those days, all he thought about was going to parties and having a good time. Whenever Toad heard that a party was being planned, no matter how far away, he got himself invited.

One day, Toad overheard a pair of flamingos talking about a party that was going to be held in the sky. "That sounds fun," said Toad. "Will you ask if I can go too?" The flamingos agreed and a few days later, an invitation arrived for Toad.

His friend Armadillo saw the invitation and was puzzled. "How will you get to a party in the sky?" she asked.

Toad smiled. "I'll find a way," he said.

The next day, Toad went to visit Buzzard, who lived nearby, and found him playing his violin. Buzzard seldom had any visitors, so he was surprised to see Toad.

"Good day, Buzzard," said Toad. "Are you going to the party in the sky?"

"Yes," said Buzzard. "All the birds are invited."

"Well, I'm invited too," said Toad. "Maybe we can go together?"

Buzzard was pleased that Toad wanted his company. "All right," he said. "What time shall we leave?"

"Come to my house at four o'clock," said Toad, "and bring your violin – everyone loves music at a party!"

On the day of the party, Buzzard arrived at Toad's house, carrying his violin case. However, Toad said that he wasn't quite ready. "Leave your violin outside by the door and come in for a moment," he said.

Buzzard put down his violin and followed Toad inside. But while Buzzard waited for him to get ready, Toad climbed out of the back window, hopped round to the front door and hid himself inside the violin case.

Buzzard waited and waited. He called out to Toad but there was no reply. Eventually he gave up. He fetched his violin, grumbling that Toad was most unreliable, and flew off to the party in the sky.

When he arrived at the party, Buzzard laid down his violin and went to find something to eat. Out hopped Toad, laughing at his trick!

Soon, Toad was having lots of fun. Buzzard was astonished to find him singing and dancing. "How did you get here?" he asked.

Toad just chuckled. "I'll tell you one day!" he said.

Toad had a wonderful time, but Buzzard didn't enjoy the party. Nobody wanted to hear him play, or dance with him, so he went home early, quite forgetting about the violin.

At the end of the party, weary Toad climbed into the violin case and waited to be carried home. But nothing happened. He began to get worried. "I wish I'd never come so far away from home!" he whimpered.

Then Falcon noticed the violin case. "That belongs to Buzzard," he said, "I'll take it to him."

At last, Toad felt himself carried through the sky. But Falcon was also weary after all the dancing. "This violin is heavier than it looks," he puffed. "Why should I bother with it, Buzzard is no friend of mine." So he let the violin drop and down to earth it fell.

Toad peered out in alarm, calling for the stones below to get out of the way. But they had deaf ears and the violin crashed to the ground and splintered into a hundred pieces.

Buzzard never knew what happened to his violin, but Toad is still covered in bumps and bruises and has quite gone off parties.

SOUTH
AMERICA

SOUTH AMERICA
A STORY FROM BRAZIL

HOW THE BEETLES GOT THEIR GORGEOUS COATS

One morning a big rat scampered out of his hole and sat in the sunshine to clean his whiskers. He noticed a little beetle, scuttling along the top of a wall.

"Hey, Beetle," he said, "how can you move so slowly? You'll never get anywhere in the world creeping along like that!"

The little beetle didn't say a word. She just kept crawling forward on her tiny feet.

"I bet you wish you could run like this," cried the rat and he darted off at great speed to the end of the wall and back again. Meanwhile, the beetle had hardly moved at all.

The rat shook the dust off his tail. "That's how to get somewhere," he chuckled. "What a pity you'll never know how it feels to move fast like me."

"You certainly can run fast, Rat," said the beetle, but she'd been taught that it wasn't polite to boast and so she didn't mention the things that she could do well.

Nearby, on the branch of a mango tree sat a green and gold parrot. She'd been listening to the exchange between the rat and the beetle with interest. "Why don't you challenge the beetle to a race?" she said to the rat. "I'll offer the winner a bright new coat made by my neighbour, the tailor bird."

The rat glanced at his dull-coloured fur. "I've always thought I'd look rather fine in a blue coat with tiger stripes," he said.

"For me it would be something shiny," said the beetle.

The rat exploded with laughter. "You'd never have a chance of winning against me!"

The beetle looked offended. "Well, you won't win either unless we have a race," she replied.

The rat grinned. "All right," he said. "Let's race!"

And so it was agreed. The parrot flew to a palm tree at the top of the cliff, which was to be the finishing line. When she gave a loud squawk the race began.

The rat scooted off as fast as he could, along the cliff path. Half way, he realised that he didn't need to hurry, so he slowed down a little to catch his breath. "Why tire myself out?" he thought, "That beetle will still be scuttling along at sunset. It's hardly worth racing her at all." But then he thought of the fancy new coat he would win, so he took off again at top speed, eager to claim his prize.

However, when he reached the palm tree at the top of the cliff, the rat couldn't believe his eyes. There was the little beetle, sitting beside the green and gold parrot.

"How did you get here so fast?" he gasped in disbelief.

The beetle drew out the tiny wings from her sides. "Nobody mentioned any rules about running," she said, "so I flew instead."

The rat stared in astonishment. "I didn't know you could fly!"

"Never judge by looks alone," said the parrot. "You don't know when you may find hidden wings."

Then the parrot asked the beetle what colours she wanted for her new coat. The beetle looked around at the green and gold palm trees and the green and gold mangos.

"I choose green and gold," she said. So, the tailor bird made the beetle a shiny new green coat with flecks of golden light in it, and the foolish rat was left to wear his dull old coat of grey.

SOUTH AMERICA

EUROPE

EUROPE
A STORY FROM DENMARK

THE NIGHTINGALE

EUROPE

There once was an Emperor of China who loved to surround himself with beautiful things. Visitors came from near and far to admire his magnificent palace and gaze at the flowers in his garden.

At the far end of the Emperor's garden was a wood that went down to the sea. There, the water was so deep that ships could sail close to the shore and pass beneath the overhanging branches, and in those branches lived a nightingale.

The nightingale delighted everyone who heard her sing. Fishermen stopped to listen to her song and travellers sailing by the wood agreed that the nightingale was more precious than anything else the Emperor possessed. It so happened that one of those travellers was a writer, who described the nightingale in a book, and one day that book was given to the Emperor.

The Emperor was astonished to read that a nightingale was more precious than anything else in his palace or his garden.

"Bring me this bird," he said. "I wish to hear her sing."

The Emperor's men couldn't find a nightingale in the palace or the garden, but at last they found a kitchen maid who had often seen the nightingale when she walked home through the wood. She was sent to ask the little bird to sing for the Emperor.

"My song would sound better among the trees," said the nightingale when she heard the Emperor's request, but she graciously agreed to come to the palace.

A perch was made for the nightingale and the whole court gathered to hear the little bird sing for the Emperor. The nightingale sang so sweetly that she touched the hearts of everyone who heard her and brought tears of joy to the Emperor's eyes.

The Emperor was delighted and offered the nightingale rich rewards. The nightingale thanked him, and explained that she was already rewarded if her song had brought tears to the eyes of an Emperor.

Then the Emperor had a golden cage made for the nightingale so that he could hear her sing every day. The nightingale was allowed to fly into the garden, but only with a silk cord fastened to her foot so that she should not fly far. Soon, everyone in the palace was talking about the wonderful bird and, before long, everyone in the city had heard about her beautiful song.

One day, a parcel arrived for the Emperor. Inside was a mechanical bird, studded with diamonds and rubies and sapphires. When the Emperor turned a little silver key, the glittering bird began to sing a tune. "This is a wonder!" marvelled the Emperor. "The two birds must sing together."

The nightingale was brought to sing with the mechanical bird. However, their voices did not sound beautiful together.

"The mechanical bird is superior," said the Emperor's clockmaker. "She will always keep perfect time and never need to rest her voice and she is so much prettier to look at than the dull little nightingale."

So the mechanical bird was put on the perch and sang her song all day for everyone in the palace.

That evening, the Emperor asked to hear the real nightingale sing once more, but she couldn't be found. Everyone had been so dazzled by the mechanical bird that they hadn't noticed her fly back to the wood.

"You have the better bird here," the clockmaker assured the Emperor. "True, the real nightingale's tune was ever-changing, but the mechanical bird is reliable; its tiny cogs and wheels will always give you the same song."

Then the Emperor had the jewelled bird placed on a silk cushion in an honoured position by his bed and, although it only sang one tune, that tune pleased him. Eventually he learned the notes and could sing along.

All was well for a year; the mechanical bird sang from morning to night without needing to rest her voice and everyone in the city loved her tune. Then, one day, there was a sudden 'bang' and she fell silent.

EUROPE

The Emperor sent for the clockmaker, who fixed the bird, but explained that some of her parts were almost worn out. "From now on she should only sing once a year," he said, "otherwise she will stop altogether."

Five years passed and the Emperor became very ill. With heavy hearts, his doctors reported that he did not have long to live. The palace began busy preparations for his successor, but they covered the floors of all the rooms with cloth, so that not a step would disturb the Emperor's peace.

Meanwhile, the Emperor lay in his room, feeling a great weight upon his heart. When he opened his eyes he saw that Death was sitting on his chest, surrounded by the scowling faces of the Emperor's bad deeds and the smiling faces of his good deeds. They all began whispering to him about the things he had done in his life.

The Emperor became very distressed. He wished that he could drown out their voices with music, but there was no one to play. He pleaded with the mechanical bird to sing her tune, but without a hand to wind her key she couldn't sing a note.

The Emperor stared into the hollow eyes of Death. Suddenly, he heard a sweet familiar song; it was the nightingale singing at his open window. She had heard of the Emperor's illness and had come to comfort him. At the sound of her pure voice, the ghostly faces began to grow pale.

The nightingale sang about the quiet churchyard where white roses bloom and Death felt a longing for his garden and retreated, like a shadow, from the room. Then the Emperor felt his strength return.

"Precious bird," he said. "You have sung away Death. How can I reward you?"

"Let me come and go freely," said the nightingale. "I shall sing to you about everything that is good and bad beyond the palace, so that you may rule with wisdom.

The Emperor gladly agreed and lived many happy years, ruling his people wisely.

EUROPE

EUROPE
A STORY FROM NORWAY

THE THREE BILLY GOATS GRUFF

Three Billy Goats Gruff were climbing over the mountainside one morning, looking for breakfast, when they spied a meadow of green, green grass.

Big Billy Goat Gruff stopped to smell the delicious grass on the breeze. Middle-sized Billy Goat Gruff stopped to lick his hungry lips, but Little Billy Goat Gruff started up the mountain path as fast as his legs could carry him.

To get to the meadow of green, green grass, Little Billy Goat Gruff had to cross a deep river and the only way to reach the other side was over a rickety wooden bridge. However, under the bridge lived a great ugly Troll, with eyes as big as saucers and a nose as long as a rolling pin.

Little Billy Goat Gruff set off, trip, trap, trip, trap, over the rickety bridge. Half way across he heard a terrible roar.

"Who dares to go trip, trap, trip, trap, over my bridge?" demanded the troll.

Little Billy Goat Gruff trembled.

"It is only I, Little Billy Goat Gruff," he answered, "on my way to eat the green, green grass in the meadow."

"A goat, eh?" chuckled the troll. "Then I'm coming to gobble you up!"

"Oh no!" cried Little Billy Goat Gruff. "There's no meat on me, I'm only skin and bone. Wait for my brother who's coming along after me – he's much fatter than I am."

The troll thought for a moment, and then he said, "All right, be off with you." Little Billy Goat Gruff hurried over the bridge and away up the path to the meadow of green, green grass.

A few minutes later, Middle-sized Billy Goat Gruff arrived and started to cross, trip, trap, trip, trap, over the rickety bridge.

"Who's that going trip, trap, trip, trap, over my bridge?" demanded the troll.

Middle-sized Billy Goat Gruff trembled.

"It is only I, Middle-sized Billy Goat Gruff," he answered.

"Then I'm coming to gobble you up!"

boomed the troll.

"Oh no," cried Middle-sized Billy Goat Gruff, "please don't eat me. If you do, you won't have room for my big brother who's coming along. He's much fatter than me."

The troll thought for a moment, and then he said, "All right, be off with you." And Middle-sized Billy Goat Gruff hurried over the bridge and away up the path to the meadow of green, green grass.

A few minutes later, Big Billy Goat Gruff arrived and started to cross, trip, trap, trip, trap, over the rickety bridge.

"Who's that going trip, trap, trip, trap, over my bridge?" demanded the troll.

Big Billy Goat Gruff stopped and snorted impatiently at the delay to his journey.

"It is I, Big Billy Goat Gruff!" he answered.

"Then I'm coming to gobble you up!" said the troll.

"You may have frightened my brothers, but you don't frighten me!" said Big Billy Goat Gruff and he stamped his hooves and lowered his horns. When the great ugly troll climbed onto the bridge, Big Billy Goat Gruff charged and tossed him high into the air. Up, up, up went the troll, then down, down, down, into the deep, cold river with a splash!

Big Billy Goat Gruff continued on his way, trip, trap, trip, trap over the rickety bridge, to join his brothers for a delicious breakfast in the meadow of green, green grass.

EUROPE

EUROPE
A STORY FROM WALES

THE OWL OF COWLYD COOMB

The Eagle of the Alder Wood had lived for many tens of years and was very old and lonely.

His wife had died long ago and his children had flown away to raise families of their own.

"I need a new wife to keep me company," Eagle thought to himself. But he didn't want the bother of raising any more children, for he was too old and tired to feed a squabbling brood again.

"If I find a new wife she must be really old like me, so that she will be happy just sitting quietly at my side."

A few days later, Eagle heard about an old owl who lived alone in a place called Cowlyd Coomb.

"Maybe she needs a companion," he thought to himself. But was she old enough to be his wife?

The eagle knew it would be impolite to ask the owl her age, so he went to see his friend, the Stag of Ferny-side Brae.

"Tell me, Stag," said Eagle, "how old is the Owl of Cowlyd Coomb?"

Stag was sitting beside a tree stump. "For hundreds of years I watched this tree grow from a little acorn into the tallest, broadest oak tree in the wood," he said. "Then, for hundreds of years, I watched it die. I can tell you that when that little acorn fell from the branch, the Owl of Cowlyd Coomb was already old. But if you want to know more, ask the Salmon of Glynllifon, she is much older than me."

The eagle thanked the stag and went to find the salmon.

"Tell me, Salmon," said Eagle, "how old is the Owl of Cowlyd Coomb?"

Salmon flapped her tail thoughtfully. "I have lived a year for every scale on my body," she said, "and for every egg in my belly. But when I was just a small fry, the Owl of Cowlyd Coomb was already old. If you want to know more, ask the Ouzel of Cilgwri, he is much older than me."

The eagle thanked the salmon and went to find the ouzel.

"Tell me, Ouzel," he asked, "how old is the Owl of Cowlyd Coomb?"

The ouzel was perched on a rock.

"See that stone at your feet, no bigger than a nut?" he said. "Well, once it was a boulder so huge that it would have needed a hundred oxen to move it. The reason it wore away is because I have wiped my beak on it every day of my long, long life. But when I was a chick in the nest, the Owl of Cowlyd Coomb was already old."

"If you want to know more, you must ask the Toad of Cors Fochno, he is the only one older than me," he continued.

The eagle thanked the ouzel and went to find the toad.

"Tell me, toad," he asked, "how old is the Owl of Cowlyd Coomb?"

Toad gazed up at the distant hills. "On this bog there once stood a hill, as high as those you see with their heads in the clouds, but I have slowly, slowly eaten it up, taking only tiny mouthfuls of dust every day. I can assure you that when I was just a tadpole, the Owl of Cowlyd Coomb was already very, very old."

Then the eagle was sure that the owl was old enough to be a suitable wife, so he went to Cowlyd Coomb and asked her to marry him.

The ancient owl had been feeling lonely too, so she agreed. And there was never a happier, quieter wedding than that of the Eagle and the Owl of Cowlyd Coomb!

EUROPE

EUROPE
A STORY
FROM SCOTLAND

KING OF THE CATS

In a lonely house in the mountains lived two brothers, Duncan and Frazer, with an old housekeeper and her cat.

One autumn afternoon, Frazer went off for a walk alone. When he wasn't home by sunset, Duncan began to worry. At supper-time Frazer still hadn't appeared, but all Duncan could do was watch and wait.

At last Frazer returned, exhausted and unable to speak. The brothers silently ate their supper and then sat before the fire, with the cat curled up on the rug.

Frazer stared into the flames, a haunted look in his eyes.

"Tell me now, what kept you out so late?" asked Duncan.

Frazer shivered, even though the fire was ablaze. "I've had a strange adventure, brother," he said. "On my way home a thick fog came down and I lost my way. I wandered blindly in the gloom until I saw a light ahead. It seemed to shine from within a great oak tree..."

Frazer paused.

"Go on," said Duncan and the cat opened an eye as if he was listening.

"I climbed up into the branches," said Frazer, "and there below me, inside the hollow trunk of the tree, I saw a candle-lit church, where a funeral was taking place…"

"Go on," urged Duncan and the cat opened his other eye.

"Well, you won't believe it," said Frazer, "but the black coffin and candles were carried by cats!"

Duncan stared in disbelief and the cat jumped to its feet.

"On the coffin was a golden crown…" said Frazer, but he got no further, for the old housekeeper's cat let out a shriek.

"Old Peter's dead!" he cried. "I'm king of the Cats!" And he rushed up the chimney and was never seen again.

EUROPE

DAPPLEGRIM

Once there was a man and his wife who had twelve sons. The youngest son, Lars, wanted to seek his fortune, so he said goodbye to his family and travelled until he came to a king's palace, where he found work in the stables.

After a year, Lars returned home, only to discover that his parents had died and all their belongings had been divided up between his brothers.

"What shall be my inheritance?" asked Lars. His brothers hadn't shared out the twelve mares grazing on the hill, so Lars took those for his own. Each mare had a foal and a big dapple-grey one caught his eye. "You are a fine fellow," said Lars.

"Yes," said the dapple-grey, "but if you kill the other foals and let me feed from all the mares you shall see how big and handsome I can grow!" Lars was curious, so he did as the foal suggested and went back to work in the palace.

When he returned, the dapple-grey had grown fat and strong, with a bright, shiny coat and all the mares had foals once more.

"Let me feed from the mares for another year," said the dapple-grey, "and you shall see how much bigger and more handsome I can grow!" So Lars did the same again.

Another year passed and the dapple-grey grew so tall that Lars couldn't reach to touch its neck and so bright that its coat glistened. Once more it asked to feed from all the mares, so Lars agreed.

The following year, the dapple-grey was so huge that it had to lie down for Lars to get on its back and its coat shone like a mirror. "Now we must go to the palace," said Dapplegrim, for that was his name.

They caused quite a commotion when they rode up to the palace, where the king was standing on the steps. "Only a noble man would ride such a magnificent horse," remarked the king and he offered Lars a position at court.

It so happened that, while Lars had been

EUROPE

95

away, the king's daughter had been carried off into the mountains by a troll. When some of the courtiers saw Lars being favoured by the king they became jealous. They told the king that they'd heard Lars boasting he could rescue the princess.

The king sent for Lars at once and insisted that he should rescue the princess or be punished. Lars knew it was useless to protest, although he was certain that he'd been given an impossible task. However, Dapplegrim assured him it could be done. "Have four strong horseshoes made for me and I will help you," he said.

When Dapplegrim had his shoes, they journeyed for several days to the mountain of the troll. The mountainside was steep and smooth as glass. At first, Dapplegrim slipped down, with a sound like thunder, but he tried and tried again. At last he sprang up the rock and into the troll's cave.

Before the troll could reach for his club, Lars swept the princess up behind him and escaped with her down the mountain.

During the long journey home, the princess and Lars fell in love. At the palace, the king greeted his daughter with joy. He was grateful to Lars, but when he heard that the princess and her brave rescuer wished to marry he turned to his courtiers for advice.

"That boy is not good enough for the princess," they muttered jealously, so the king set Lars another task.

The palace was overshadowed by a huge hill that prevented the sun from shining in.

"If you can bring sunshine into the palace you shall marry my daughter," said the king.

Lars felt his heart sink. "I'll do my best," he promised and he went to tell Dapplegrim about the task.

"Have four new horseshoes made for me," said Dapplegrim, "and I will help you." When the shoes were made, Lars rode Dapplegrim to the top of the hill. Then the huge horse stamped his heavy feet and flattened it. Sunshine flooded into the palace.

"Now you must agree to let us marry, Father," said the princess, but once more the

EUROPE

king listened to his courtiers, who advised him to set Lars another task.

"If you wish to marry my daughter," said the king, "you must find her a horse as magnificent as yours to ride to the wedding."

Lars was sure that there could be no other horse like Dapplegrim. "There is one," said Dapplegrim, "but he lives underground and will not be easy to catch." Then he told Lars to fetch 12 barrels of corn, 12 barrels of meat, a barrel of tar and 12 ox hides studded with spikes.

Lars gathered everything and set off on Dapplegrim, but they had not gone far when all the wild birds of the forest flew out to stop them. Dapplegrim told Lars to spill the corn from the barrels and the birds flew down to eat.

A little farther on, all the wild beasts of the forests came out to stop them, but Lars threw them the meat from the barrels and they were able to escape.

On they went, until they came to a wild heath. There, Dapplegrim stopped and neighed loudly. He was answered from beneath the ground. Quickly, he told Lars to cover him with the ox hides and pour the tar from the barrel.

Out of the earth galloped a magnificent horse, breathing flames from its nostrils. At once the tar caught fire and the two horses began to fight. "If the flames rise, I have won," cried Dapplegrim, "if they sink, I have failed." The fight was fierce, but Dapplegrim was so well protected that he couldn't be harmed. Lars watched the flames rise until the strange horse finally gave up the fight and Lars slipped a bridle around his neck.

The two horses were identical. When the king saw that Lars had done everything he'd asked, while his courtiers had done nothing but complain, he dismissed them all. Lars and the Princess were wed at last and they both lived happily ever after.

EUROPE

EUROPE
A STORY FROM SCOTLAND

THE EAGLE AND THE WREN

The birds of the mountains and the sea, the forests and the moorland, gathered one day to choose themselves a queen. But although they talked for many hours, they found it impossible to agree; some wanted Eagle to be their queen and others wanted Wren.

"Why not decide with a test?" suggested Wren. "Whichever one of us can fly the highest shall be queen."

The other birds thought this was a strange suggestion from the little Wren, but as they were all tired of arguing they agreed.

So the two birds took flight. Wren fluttered straight up on her tiny wings while Eagle stretched out her fine long feathers and soared in great circles. When Wren had risen as high as she could go, she dropped down lightly onto Eagle's back.

Eagle flew higher and higher, until the other birds watching below could only see a small speck among the mountain peaks. At last, she could rise no more, so she glided gracefully down to the ground.

"Eagle flew the highest!" said the birds. "She shall be our queen."

To everyone's surprise, a tiny head peeped out of the feathers on Eagle's back.

"No, it should be me!" chirped Wren. "I hid here until Eagle could rise no more and then I flapped my wings and flew a moment higher."

Wren's words caused much twittering and warbling and clucking and hooting, but this time everyone did agree.

"You didn't reach the mountain peaks yourself, Wren," said Owl. "Eagle flew the highest and she did so carrying you on her back." Then all the birds cheered for Eagle, their new queen.

Wren crept away but she learned wisdom that day, for she never flew far from the earth again or tried to be what she was not.

EUROPE

EUROPE

A STORY FROM IRELAND

SAINT DOMNOC AND THE BEES

EUROPE

Domnoc was descended from the royal family of O'Neil in Ireland, but he decided to leave his native country to become a monk.

He sailed to Wales, where he found a place at the monastery of David. David taught Domnoc and took him into his care and when he wasn't studying or praying, Domnoc helped with the work at the monastery. Rather than cook or clean, Domnoc chose to work in the garden and was given responsibility for the bees, which the monks kept so that they had honey to give to the poor.

Domnoc loved the gentle, busy bees. He learned their habits and looked after their beehives. Before long, he noticed which flowers the bees loved best and planted them around the garden. As Domnoc went about his work, weeding the flowerbeds or tending the vegetables, he talked to the bees, who buzzed about him as if to keep him company.

The monastery bees were so well looked after that they made plenty of honey for the poor and Domnoc thanked God for his tiny friends.

After several years of study, Domnoc was ready to return home to Ireland as a monk. He was sad to be leaving his wise teacher, David, and all his friends at the monastery, and also sorry to have to say goodbye to his little companions, the bees. When he went down to the beehives for the last time, they gathered around him, as if they knew he was going away.

"Keep doing God's work, my friends," said Domnoc, and he left to board his ship, waiting in the harbour.

Domnoc boarded the ship, but before the crew could set sail they heard a strange humming sound. Out of the sky flew a great swarm of bees that came to rest upon the sail.

Domnoc knew at once that they had come from the monastery. "Go home, my friends," he told them. "You have important work to do, making honey for the poor." But the bees would not leave Domnoc, so he had to lead them back to the monastery himself.

Domnoc explained to David what had happened and when the bees were in their hives once more, he returned to the ship and set sail across the Irish Sea. However, the crew soon noticed a hazy black cloud following the ship.

"The bees are coming!" they cried in alarm. Despite the lively wind, the bees struggled on until they reached the ship and settled on the sail once more.

"They've come so far on their tiny wings, they'll never be able to fly home," said Domnoc. "We must sail back to Wales."

Reluctantly, the crew turned around and when they reached the shore, Domnoc led the bees back to the monastery again.

David watched Domnoc settling the bees back into their hives. "These bees wish to be with you, Domnoc," he said. "Take a basket with you on the ship this time. If they follow you again you must accept them with my blessing."

Domnoc thanked his teacher and took a basket back to the ship.

Sure enough, the bees followed Domnoc for the third time. When they reached the ship they were so weak and tired that they came to rest on the deck. "Don't be afraid," Domnoc told the crew and he gently gathered the bees into the basket, where they stayed for the rest of the voyage.

Home at last in Ireland, Domnoc set up a new church and planted a garden full of flowers. There, he taught others to live gentle, busy lives, providing for the poor, just like the bees.

EUROPE

EUROPE
AN ENGLISH STORY

THE THREE LITTLE PIGS

O nce upon a time, there were three little pigs, called Snuffle, Spot and Curly. Snuffle liked to eat all day, Spot loved a long snooze, but their sister Curly was always busy with clever ideas.

As the little pigs grew bigger, their house became quite a squeeze. So, one day, they decided it was time to build houses of their own.

The three little pigs set out together.

Before long, Snuffle stopped by the wood to eat some blackberries. When he was full, he looked around for something to build his house with. "There are plenty of sticks here," he thought, so he built himself a house of sticks.

Further down the lane, Spot found a pile of straw and stopped for a nap. When he woke up, he looked around for something to build his house with. "Straw is comfy," he thought, so he built himself a house of straw.

Meanwhile, Curly walked on until she found a pile of bricks. "These are perfect for strong walls," she thought, so she built herself a house of bricks.

The next day, a big, bad wolf tramped out of the wood.

He saw the stick house and smelled a little pig inside.

"Little pig, little pig, let me come in," he said in a tiny voice.

But Snuffle spotted the wolf's tail through the window.

"No!" he cried. "I won't let you in. Not by the hair on my chinny-chin-chin!"

"Then I'll huff and I'll puff and I'll blow your house down!" bellowed the wolf and he took a deep breath and blew...

Snuffle ran out of the back door and down the lane as fast as his little legs could carry him. He came to Spot's house.

EUROPE

"Help," he shouted, "the wolf is coming!" Spot opened the door and let him in.

Before Snuffle could catch his breath, along came the big, bad wolf.

He saw the straw house and smelled the little pigs inside.

"Little pigs, little pigs, let me come in," said the wolf.

"No!" cried Spot. "We won't let you in. Not by the hair on our chinny-chin-chins!"

"Then I'll huff and I'll puff and I'll blow your house down!" bellowed the wolf and he took a deep breath and blew...

Snuffle and Spot ran out of the back door and down the lane as fast as their little legs could carry them, until they came to Curly's house.

"Help," they shouted, "the wolf is coming!" Curly opened the door and they hurried inside.

Before Snuffle and Spot could catch their breath, along came the big, bad wolf.

He saw the brick house and smelled the little pigs inside.

"Little pigs, little pigs, let me come in!" said the wolf.

"No!" cried Curly. "We won't let you in. Not by the hair on our chinny-chin-chins!"

"Then I'll huff and I'll puff and I'll blow your house down!" bellowed the wolf and he took a deep breath and blew...

But nothing happened! The wolf huffed and puffed until his face was red, but he couldn't blow down a house of bricks.

"Hurray, we're safe!" cried the three little pigs.

However, a moment later, they heard footsteps on the roof. Curly thought fast and put a pan of water to boil on the stove.

The three little pigs held their breath as the big, bad wolf began to lower himself down the chimney...

A tail appeared and then...SPLASH! He fell into the boiling water! The big bad wolf let out a mighty howl. Up he jumped, out he ran and he was never seen again.

And the three little pigs lived together happily ever after.

EUROPE

EUROPE
A STORY
FROM FINLAND

MIGHTY MIKKO

Once there was an old woodsman who had come to the end of his days. He called his son, Mikko, to his bedside.

"You are a good, kind young man, Mikko," he said. "I have nothing to leave you except this humble cottage and the three snares I've used for many years to catch animals in the forest. When I am dead, go into the forest and inspect the snares. If you find a wild creature trapped there, bring it home alive."

The old woodsman died shortly afterwards and Mikko followed his father's advice. Sure enough, he found a little red fox trapped in one of the snares. Mikko gently freed the fox and carried it home, where he bandaged its bruised foot and gave it food from his own dish. When its foot was healed, the fox stayed with Mikko and they became friends.

One day the fox noticed that Mikko was lonely. "You need a wife to keep you company," he said.

Mikko smiled sadly. "I have nothing to offer a wife. Who would want to live in this humble cottage?"

"You are a good, kind young man," said the fox, "and handsome too, although you have no mirror to see it! The princess at the palace couldn't ask for more."

"You're making fun of me!" Mikko laughed. "It's true, I am lonely and they say the princess is loved by everyone who meets her, but she would never look at a poor boy like me."

"We shall see," said the fox and he went off to visit the king.

When he was shown into the throne room, the fox made a gracious bow. "I bring greetings from my master," he said. "He asks if your Highness would lend him a barrel."

"That's an odd request!" exclaimed the king. "Who is your master and why does he want it?"

The fox put on an air of great importance.

"You must have heard of my master, the Mighty Mikko?" he said.

The king frowned. He had never heard the name, but he didn't want to appear ill informed. "Oh yes, Mighty Mikko." He nodded knowingly. "And why does he want to borrow a barrel?"

"My master wants to send a small gift to his bootmaker," said the fox. "He promises to return the barrel tomorrow." The king was curious and so he agreed.

On his way home, the fox stopped at the market, where he hunted beneath the stalls for all the coins that had been dropped that day.

The next morning, he pushed the coins into the cracks in the barrel and returned it to the king. The king noticed the glinting coins at once. "This fellow, Mighty Mikko, must be very wealthy if he gives a barrel of coins to his bootmaker," he thought, so he asked the fox if his master would visit the palace.

The fox shook his head. "That's impossible, I'm afraid," he said. "My master wishes to marry and has been invited by several foreign kings to meet their daughters. Tomorrow he sets off on his journey."

When the king heard this he thought of his own daughter, who was loved by everyone who met her, but had never fallen in love herself. "Ask your master to come here first," he said. "We will make him very welcome."

The fox sighed and stepped close to whisper in the king's ear, as if he didn't want the servants to hear. "I'm afraid your palace isn't big enough to entertain my Master and all the men he travels with," he said.

The king was astounded. "Mighty Mikko must be truly noble to have such a huge company of men," he thought. "If only he would agree to come here, he might be a perfect husband for the princess."

The fox pretended to leave, but as he reached the door of the throne room he hesitated. "I'm sure my Master would like to return your kindness for lending him the barrel," he said.

EUROPE

"Sometimes he travels around the land in disguise, dressed as a humble woodsman…"

"Then bid him come as a woodsman," said the king eagerly. "When he is here I will give him my finest clothes to wear."

Hiding a smile, the fox thanked the king and trotted home to Mikko.

Mikko was amazed to hear about the king's invitation. The following day, he went with the fox to the palace, where he was given a great welcome by the king and dressed in the finest clothes.

As the fox had predicted, Mikko's handsome face and good, kind nature soon won the heart of the Princess and, like everyone who met her, he fell in love too. Nobody was happier than the king himself, and before long Mikko and the Princess were married with his blessing.

All went well, until the king asked to visit Mikko's castle, to see where his daughter would make her new home.

Mikko was worried that his new happiness would quickly come to an end. "Leave everything to me," said the fox. "A day's ride from here is a beautiful castle, inhabited by a wicked old dragon called the Worm. Travel there with the king and ask any one you see along the way to tell you who their master is." Mikko didn't like the sound of the Worm but he trusted his

faithful friend and so he agreed.

The fox set off ahead of the others, towards the castle of the Worm. On the way he met ten farmers ploughing the Worm's fields. "A great king is coming to kill your master," he told them. "If you want to save yourselves, tell him that your master is Mighty Mikko." The farmers thanked him and he continued on his way.

A little farther on, the fox met 20 shepherds, tending the Worm's sheep and he told them the same thing.

On he went to the castle, where the old Worm was counting his gold. The fox pretended to be afraid and told the Worm that he was running from the battle that was about to begin. "What battle?" asked the Worm in alarm.

"A great king is coming to kill you," said the fox, "and he brings a thousand men!"

The Worm knew that his fighting days were over. "I'll reward you with gold if you help me to hide," he said hurriedly. "Lock me in the gardener's shed; the king will never find me there."

The fox obliged and locked the wicked old Worm in the shed – and then he burned it to the ground!

Meanwhile, the royal party met the farmers and the shepherds who all told the king that their master was Mighty Mikko.

When they reached the castle, the fox was there to welcome Mikko and his bride to their magnificent new home.

EUROPE

EUROPE
A STORY FROM FRANCE

THE SPECKLED HEN

EUROPE

One day, a speckled hen was scratching around for worms when she noticed something lumpy, half-buried in the ground. As she scraped away at it, the miller came along the road. "Silly bird," he scoffed. "What a waste of time scratching in the ground like that!"

"Not at all," said the speckled hen and with one tug of her beak she pulled out a purse, which fell open, spilling ten gold coins on the ground at her feet. "That was time well spent!" she said.

The miller eyed the gold coins. "What a bit of luck. Ten gold coins is just what I need. Lend them to me and I'll return them in eight days." The speckled hen was a kind bird. "Very well," she said and she gave the coins to the miller.

Eight days passed but there was no sign of the miller. The speckled hen realised that her coins would not be returned. "I shall go to the miller's house and get those ten gold coins back myself," she said.

Along the way, she met a ladder by the side of the road.

"Where are you going, Speckled Hen?" asked the ladder.

"I'm going to see the miller, who owes me ten gold coins. Will you come with me?"

"Yes!" said the ladder.

"Very well, get inside of me," said the speckled hen and the ladder jumped down her throat.

A little further on, she came to a river.

"Where are you going, Speckled Hen?" asked the river.

"I'm going to see the miller, who owes me ten gold coins. Will you come with me?"

"Yes!" said the river.

"Very well, get inside of me," said the speckled hen and the river jumped down her throat.

The speckled hen walked on, into the wood. There she met a wolf.

"Where are you going, Speckled Hen?" asked the wolf.

"I'm going to see the miller, who owes me ten gold coins. Will you come with me?"

"Yes!" said the wolf.

"Very well, get inside of me," said the speckled hen and the wolf jumped down her throat.

The speckled hen walked on until she came to the miller's house. She marched straight inside and asked the miller for her ten gold coins.

The miller just laughed. "I knew you were a silly bird!" And he seized the speckled hen, carried her outside and threw her into the well.

The speckled hen thought fast. "Ladder, ladder, come out of me!" she cried. At once the ladder jumped out of her throat and the speckled hen climbed out of the well.

She marched back to the house and asked again for her ten gold coins.

The miller was angry when he saw that the speckled hen had escaped. He grabbed her with both hands and threw her into his oven.

The speckled hen thought fast. "River, river, come out of me!" she cried. At once, the river jumped out of her throat. It put out the oven fire, burst open the door and the speckled hen bobbed out.

"I won't be made a fool of!" shouted the miller and he snatched up the speckled hen, took her out to the stable and threw her among the oxen's heavy feet.

The speckled hen thought fast.

"Wolf, wolf, come out of me!" she cried. At once, the wolf jumped out of her throat. He chased the oxen out of the stable and then he chased the miller over the hill and far away.

The speckled hen soon found her ten gold coins under the miller's bed.

"That was time well spent," she said happily and off she went home.

EUROPE

EUROPE
A SPANISH STORY

THE WHITE PARROT

Mariquita lived with her father and her brother, in a beautiful house with a pretty courtyard full of flowers. One morning, Mariquita was watering the flowers and singing happily to herself, when she noticed an old woman at the gate.

"Is your father home?" asked the old woman.

"No," answered Mariquita.

"Is your brother home?"

Mariquita shook her head. The old woman peered through the gate. "What a charming courtyard," she said.

"Would you like to see it?" asked Mariquita proudly. She opened the gate and welcomed her in.

The old woman admired Mariquita's beautiful flowers. "Very pretty," she said, "but what you need is a fountain of silver water."

"How wonderful!" sighed Mariquita. "Where can I find such a thing?"

"I will tell you the place," said the old woman. "If you fill a jug from the fountain there and put it in your courtyard, it will become a fountain of silver water."

When Mariquita's father and brother returned, she told them about the fountain and wouldn't stop asking for one until her brother agreed to go in search of it.

He took a jug and set off. Far from home he met an old man.

"Who hates you so much to send you here?" asked the old man.

The boy explained that he was searching for a fountain of silver water.

"That's a dangerous task," said the old man, "but you may succeed. The fountain is guarded by a great lion. Take care! If his eyes are closed, he can see you, but if his eyes are open, then he is fast asleep."

The boy thanked the old man and walked on until he found the fountain. There, lying beside it, was a great lion. He waited until the lion's eyes were open, filled the jug and hurried home.

Mariquita stood the jug in the courtyard and it became a beautiful fountain of silver water, just as the old woman had promised. It was the loveliest thing she'd ever seen!

The next day, when her father and brother were out, the old woman passed by again. Mariquita showed her the fountain.

"That's a great improvement," said the old woman, "but you really need a tree with leaves of silver and nuts of gold."

At once, Mariquita had to have one.

When her brother returned he saw there would be no peace until he agreed to go in search of it.

Once more, he met the old man and asked for help.

"Take that horse grazing by the path," said the old man, "it will carry you into the forest where there is a tree guarded by a deadly serpent. Wait until the serpent hides his head in his coils to sleep and then break off a branch. If you plant it, the branch will grow into a tree with leaves of silver and nuts of gold."

The boy did exactly as the old man told him and took a branch home to his sister.

Sure enough, when Mariquita planted the branch in the courtyard, it grew into a beautiful tree with leaves of silver and nuts of gold.

Mariquita was delighted. "Now our courtyard is the prettiest in town," she said.

A few days later, the old woman returned.

"That is a fine tree," said the old woman. "All you need now is a white parrot."

"A white parrot?" Mariquita gasped. "Oh yes, I must have one." For the third time, she pleaded with her brother until he promised to fetch it for her.

The boy set off, not knowing where to look for a white parrot, until he met the old man again.

"This is your most dangerous task,"

EUROPE

111

warned the old man. "Follow the path until you come to a beautiful garden. There, you will see a white parrot. Wait until it settles on a branch and puts its head under its wing to sleep, and then you may take it. But beware – if you touch the white parrot before it's asleep you will be turned to stone!"

The boy walked on until he found the beautiful garden. Swooping through the trees was a dazzling white parrot. The boy gazed in amazement. As soon as the parrot settled on a branch and began to tuck its head under its wing the boy reached out for it. But, alas, he was too impatient. As his fingers touched the parrot he was turned to stone!

At home, Mariquita waited anxiously for her brother. When he didn't return, she realised how foolish she'd been to send him away.

"I shouldn't have listened to that old woman," she cried. "I'd rather have my brother home than a courtyard full of white parrots!"

So, she set off to find him. Along the path, she met the old man.

"Your brother faced many dangers for you," he said, "but if you are brave you may save him." He told Mariquita what to do.

Mariquita soon found the beautiful garden. There, to her horror, she saw her brother turned to stone. The white parrot flew out of the trees and perched on his hand. Mariquita remembered the old man's warning. She waited patiently until she was sure it was asleep, and then she reached out… as her fingers touched the white parrot her brother came to life!

Mariquita hugged him tight. "I shall never be discontent again!" she promised and they set off for home for a happy reunion with their father.

EUROPE

THE UGLY DUCKLING

One summer, Mother Duck had six fluffy yellow ducklings, but when the last egg in the nest cracked open, out tumbled an odd, grey duckling with a long neck.

The other birds in the farmyard laughed at him. "You're an ugly duckling!" they said. "You don't belong here."

Mother Duck told them not to be unkind, but while she was looking after the rest of her brood the other birds pecked at the grey duckling and made his life miserable.

One day, he ran under the hedge to hide, disturbing a flock of sparrows. "I must be ugly," he thought. "Even the sparrows fly away from me because they're afraid!" The ugly duckling felt so unhappy that he decided to run away.

Blinking back his tears, he waddled off across the fields and meadows until he came to a marsh, where he met a family of wild ducks.

"What an ugly duckling!" exclaimed the wild ducks. "You don't belong in our family."

The ugly duckling crept away into the reeds. "It seems I don't belong anywhere," he sighed.

The next day, he left the marsh and walked on until he came to a lake. None of the birds there made him welcome, so the ugly duckling was left to find a home among the water weeds alone.

Autumn came and the weather grew colder. One day, a pair of beautiful swans flew out over the lake. As the ugly duckling stared at their dazzling white feathers and elegant necks, a feeling of happiness flooded through him.

"I wish I could be as beautiful as those birds and fly with them on huge white wings," he sighed. But the swans soon disappeared beyond the woods and he was left alone once more on the grey, windy lake.

Autumn turned to winter. The lake froze and the ugly duckling shivered among the frosty reeds, with nobody to help him find

EUROPE

food and shelter from the icy north wind.

Just when he began to lose hope that winter would ever end, the lake began to melt and the ugly duckling felt the warmth of the sun on his back. Spring had arrived. He preened his feathers and stretched his wings. To his surprise, they had grown strong over the winter. The ugly duckling ran, raised his wings and swooped up into the air. "I'm flying!" he cried excitedly, although there was nobody to hear.

He flew once around the lake and then onwards, to explore what lay beyond. Down below he soon saw a sparkling river and there, to his delight, were the beautiful white birds he had admired in the autumn, gliding through the water with their heads held proud. The ugly duckling landed on the riverbank and watched them shyly, but the swans had seen him.

"Come, swim with us," they called.

The ugly duckling looked around, thinking they had spoken to somebody else, but there was no other bird nearby.

"Who, me?" he said. "I don't belong here, I'm just an ugly duckling."

"Come into the water," said the swans.

The ugly duckling stepped timidly into the water and the swans glided over to greet him. "Look at your reflection," they said.

He looked at his reflection. A beautiful white bird stared back at him, with a fine curving neck and dazzling white wings.

"What has happened to me?" said the ugly duckling in astonishment.

His companions smiled. "You were never an ugly duckling," they said, "you were a cygnet and now you have become a swan."

The beautiful swan was no longer ashamed. "I am a swan!" he cried. Great happiness flooded through him. At last he knew where he belonged.

EUROPE

AUSTRALIA AND OCEANIA

AUSTRALIA & OCEANIA
A STORY FROM AUSTRALIA

HOW THE KANGAROO GOT HER POUCH

Kangaroo was watching her little joey play one day when an old wombat appeared, wandering blindly through the grass.

"I'm so weak," he moaned. "I'm so thirsty and hungry. I haven't a friend in the world."

Kangaroo felt sorry for the old wombat. "I'll be your friend," she said. "I'll lead you down to the creek to drink and find you some tasty grass."

She told the blind old wombat to take hold of her tail and warned her joey to stay close, as her arms were too small to carry him. Then Kangaroo led the wombat slowly down to the creek.

The joey followed, but he was full of curiosity and forgot to stay close to his mother. While the wombat enjoyed a long drink and some tasty grass, Kangaroo looked around for her joey but he was nowhere to be seen.

At that moment she spotted a hunter nearby. Kangaroo realised that the defenceless wombat was in danger.

She stamped her feet to attract the hunter's attention and then bounded off into the bush to lead him away from the defenseless wombat.

The hunter followed Kangaroo for a great distance until at last, exhausted, he gave up the hunt.

Kangaroo returned to the creek, relieved to find her joey asleep under a gum tree. But the wombat had vanished. To her surprise, the Sky Spirits appeared.

"Our Sky Father came here as a wombat to find out which creature had the kindest heart," they explained. "You alone cared for him, so he has sent you this present." And they gave Kangaroo an apron made of eucalyptus bark. When Kangaroo tied it around her waist it became a pouch to carry her joey!

Such was the Sky Father's pleasure, that every kangaroo mother has had the same pouch as a gift ever since.

AUSTRALIA & OCEANIA
A STORY FROM HAWAII

NANAUE, THE SHARK BOY

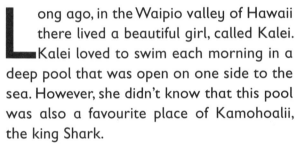

Long ago, in the Waipio valley of Hawaii there lived a beautiful girl, called Kalei. Kalei loved to swim each morning in a deep pool that was open on one side to the sea. However, she didn't know that this pool was also a favourite place of Kamohoalii, the king Shark.

One day, as Kamohoalii swam towards the pool he noticed Kalei diving from the rocks into the water. He held back to watch, admiring her beauty and skill as she gracefully entered the water without a splash. Wishing not to frighten her, he turned away, but he came back the following morning to watch Kalei swim again, hiding at the shadowy edge of the pool so she wouldn't see him.

Day after day Kamohoalii came to gaze at Kalei and before long he fell in love with her and wanted her to be his wife.

As he possessed the power of a god, Kamohoalii transformed himself into a handsome young man and waited for Kalei on the beach. When she approached, he raised a gigantic wave to crash upon the shore. Kalei ran from the terrifying wave but just as it threatened to sweep her out to sea, Kamohoalii ran forward and rescued her. Kalei was grateful to the handsome stranger and from that moment they became friends. Every morning they walked and swam together and, before long, she too had fallen in love and they were married.

Kalei and her husband lived happily together by the sea until, one day, she told him she was expecting a child. Then Kamohoalii knew it was time to tell her about his true nature. Kalei was afraid when she heard that her husband was the powerful god, King Shark, but her love for him was strong.

"If I stay here our family will be in danger," he told her, "so I must return to my people. I will always love and protect you and I will make a safe place for our child to play at the bottom of the pool."

When the day of the birth was close, Kamohoalii gave Kalei a feather cape for the child to wear and warned her never to let him eat meat or it would bring tradegy on the village. Then they said their sad goodbyes and Kalei watched her husband walk into the sea and disappear under the waves.

A short while later, their son was born and she called him Nanaue. He was a healthy normal boy, but on his back, between his shoulder blades, was the mouth of a shark. Then Kalei knew why her husband had given her the cloak.

Kalei kept her son's extraordinary birthmark a secret from everyone in the village. Nanaue grew up always wearing the cloak to cover his back, except when he swam in the pool by the sea, where Kalei often saw Kamohoalii in the shadows, watching over them both.

While he was a child, Nanaue never ate meat with his mother, but one day his grandfather told Nanaue that he had reached the age when it was traditional to eat with the other men of the village. Kalei couldn't protest without revealing her son's secret, so Nanaue began to eat his meals with the other men. There, his grandfather fed him plenty of meat to make

him strong and he soon became famous for his big appetite.

"Eat up quickly," the older men would say to each other, "here comes Nanaue, as ravenous as a shark!"

Meanwhile, people often wondered why Nanaue never removed his cape and never took part in village games, preferring to work alone on his mother's vegetable patch. Sometimes the other boys met Nanaue as they walked down to the sea and asked him to join them, but he always refused and warned them to take care.

Then Nanaue's grandfather died and strange things began to happen. People swimming in the sea came home with shark bites. Some of those who went met Nanaue on their way to the beach never returned.

King Shark had always forbidden his people to harm the villagers, but now they became afraid of the water.

One day, Umi, the King of Hawaii, sent an order for every man in Waipio to work for ten days on his plantation. All the men of the valley went to work for the king, except Nanaue who was afraid his secret would be discovered. But when King Umi heard about Nanaue he sent for him and put him to work.

AUSTRALIA
AND OCEANIA

Although the work was hard and the sun burned down, Nanaue kept the feather cape over his back.

The other young men teased him. "Isn't it hot enough for you, Nanaue?" they cried and one of them boldly tugged at the cape, which slipped off Nanaue's shoulders, revealing the shark mouth on his back. Everyone stared in horror.

"He's a child of King Shark!" they cried. "That's why our people have been disappearing!"

Nanaue ran off through the plantation and the men chased after him. He ran on through the valley with the strength and stamina of the shark people, until he reached the deep pool where he dived into the water before anyone could catch him.

When the men got to the pool they threw rocks into the water, but Nanaue was safe in the place that his father had made for him and when they gave up and left, he took the form of a shark and swam out to sea.

Then the villagers brought Kalei before the king. "She must be punished for bringing tragedy to our valley," they said.

But wise King Umi listened to Kalei's story. He heard how Nanaue's father had tried to protect them by forbidding his son from eating meat and he shook his head. "I see this tragedy was the grandfather's fault," he said. "Kalei should not be punished for the love of her husband and child."

So Kalei was left to live peacefully by the sea, where she often saw a pair of sharks swim together and remembered Nanaue and his loving father, Kamohoalii.

AUSTRALIA
AND OCEANIA

AUSTRALIA & OCEANIA
A STORY FROM NEW ZEALAND

PAIKEA AND RUATAPU

Long ago in Hawaiki, the ancestral homeland of the Māori people, there lived a chief called Uenuku who had many wives. Over time, his wives gave him seventy-one sons. Seventy of these sons had mothers of noble birth and the eldest of these was Kahutia-te-rangi. However, the youngest son, Ruatapu, was the child of a slave wife Uenuku had taken captive after a battle.

One day Uenuku decided to have a magnificent canoe built for his sons, beautifully carved and painted red. When the canoe was finished, he called his sons together.

"Here is my gift," he said. "But before you take up your paddles I will comb your hair with the sacred comb of our people, and tie it in the traditional way, so that everyone shall know of your noble birth."

Uenuku's sons thanked their father and knelt before him, one by one, to have their hair combed. Last in line was Ruatapu.

When he saw Ruatapu, Uenuku laid the comb down. "This is not for you," he said.

"But I'm your son, too, just like the others," said Ruatapu, feeling the eyes of his brothers upon him.

"Your mother is a slave wife," said his father. "You are not a son of noble birth, Ruatapu. You may take your place in the canoe but you have no right to be honoured with the sacred comb."

Ruatapu felt ashamed at being rejected by his father in front of his older brothers. Burning with anger, he ran away to hide.

That night Ruatapu planned his revenge. While everyone was asleep, he crept down to the water's edge, drilled a hole in the bottom of the canoe and plugged it with wood chips.

The next day a ceremony was held to launch the canoe. Ruatapu took his place and paddled out to sea with his brothers. But as soon as they were beyond sight of land, he knocked the

wood chips out of the hole with his heel. At once, the canoe began to fill with water.

Uenuku's sons searched frantically for the bailer to scoop out the water, not knowing that Ruatapu had thrown it out of the canoe.

Ruatapu took advantage of the confusion. He pushed his brothers into the sea and beat them with his paddle. Every one of them was drowned, except Kahutia-te-rangi who kept out of his reach.

"You will not drown me, Ruatapu," cried Kahutia-te-rangi. "Porpoise and whale are my ancestors. I am descended from Tangaroa, the god of the sea!" Then he called out to Tangaroa to save him.

Suddenly the water darkened and the sea heaved. A pod of whales surfaced, shooting spume and spray into the air. Kahutia-te-rangi climbed onto the back of a whale, his wet skin glistening in the sun, and it carried him away.

Ruatapu was furious to see his brother escape. "Rise up, waves," he chanted. "Follow the whale-rider and drown him like the others." Then five towering waves arose and rolled across the sea after Kahutia-te-rangi.

Kahutia-te-rangi rode the whale with such strength and skill that it seemed as if they had become one. However, instead of heading for Hawaiki, they travelled to a new land.

When they reached the shore, Kahutia-te-rangi slipped off the whale's back and stepped onto the beach. Just as he did so, Ruatapu's waves came crashing onto the sand. But instead of drowning him, they rolled over and rushed back across the sea, to drown Ruatapu himself.

From that day, Kahutia-te-rangi took the name Paikea, which means 'whale'. In time, he became the father of two tribes, and the land of the whale-rider is now known as New Zealand.

AUSTRALIA
AND OCEANIA

AUSTRALIA & OCEANIA
A STORY FROM AUSTRALIA

EMU AND THE BRUSH TURKEY

Long ago, in Dreamtime, Emu had the strongest wings and could fly far across the plains. Brush Turkey, whose flight was clumsy and weak, was jealous of Emu's wings.

One day, Brush Turkey thought of a way to trick Emu. She sat in the grass, with her own wings tucked out of sight. When Emu flew down to peck for worms, Brush Turkey sighed loudly.

"What a pity you have to carry those heavy wings around, Emu," she said.

"Anyone can fly – clever birds walk these days."

Emu looked puzzled. "But I've seen you fly," she said.

"Not any more," said Brush Turkey.

Emu walked away. "My wings are certainly heavy," she thought. "Maybe Brush Turkey is right." So she clipped her wings to make herself lighter.

The next day, when Brush Turkey saw Emu she spread her wings and flew up into a tree. "Now I have the strongest wings!" she boasted, and Emu realised that she'd been tricked.

A few days later, Emu hid ten of her chicks under a bush and took just two of them for a walk past Brush Turkey's nest.

"How foolish to feed twelve chicks," she said loudly. "With only two to feed mine will grow much bigger and stronger."

"But you have lots of chicks," said Brush Turkey.

"Not anymore," replied Emu.

Brush Turkey looked at her hungry brood. "Maybe Emu is right," she thought, so she chased ten of her chicks away.

Next day, Emu returned with all her little ones together. "A clever bird knows that her strength is not in her wings, Brush Turkey," she said, "but in the family around her!"

And that is why emus cannot fly and brush turkeys lay only two eggs.

AUSTRALIA & OCEANIA
A STORY FROM PAPUA NEW GUINEA

HOW THE FLYING FISH LIVED IN A TREE

In the old days, all the land was dry. The sea was held like an enormous raindrop in the branches of a gigantic tree, but nobody knew it was there.

In a village nearby, lived an old woman called Kemiana, who relied on her husband to take care of her. One day, as usual, her husband went out hunting, but didn't catch anything to eat. He was about to return home empty-handed when he realised that his dog was missing. The old man retraced his steps and found his dog under a tree, eating something wet and shiny.

"You seem to be enjoying that strange food," he said, "maybe it will be good for Kemiana." He didn't know that his dog was eating a flying fish that had fallen out of a hole in the sea.

The man brought some flying fish home and cooked them for Kemiana, who ate them gratefully and then fell into a deep sleep.

The next morning she didn't wake up and her husband grew worried that the flying fish had made her ill. He called in his neighbours. "I gave my wife a strange food and now I fear that she will never wake up," he said anxiously.

The neighbours gathered around Kemiana's bed and began to weep because they thought that she was dying. But suddenly she opened her eyes and smiled. "I have never slept so well, husband," she said. "Bring me more of that wonderful food."

News of the new food soon spread around the local villages. Everyone wanted to try it. However, the waves of the sea only washed a few flying fish out of the hole each day and there was not enough to feed everyone, so the men of the two local tribes decided to cut the gigantic tree down.

First, the men of the Aurana tribe chopped at the tree, while the men of the Lavarata tribe prepared food. But when the Aurana men rested and sat down to eat, the Lavarata men tricked them and kept on chopping until the tree came crashing down.

Then the great bubble of the sea burst with a terrific roar, spilling out a torrent of foamy water, alive with fins and tails and tentacles, which spread across the low land to become the ocean. All the Aurana men were washed away in the flood, doomed to become seafolk forever.

Many fish rushed into the sea that day, but the flying fish stayed behind in the swamp. It wasn't long before the village women discovered that they could catch them easily there. They stopped working on their vegetable gardens and spent their days at the swamp filling their baskets with flying fish instead.

When the men saw their vegetables choked with weeds they weren't happy. "How can we encourage our wives to give up fishing and tend to the garden?" they sighed.

An old man came forward.

"I will send the fish away into the ocean," he said, "but you must promise only to catch them there in season and share them fairly among you."

The men agreed to the old man's wishes and followed him down to the swamp, where he called out to the flying fish. "It is time for you to leave this place, fish that fly. Rise up and return to your home in the great blue belly of the sea."

Then he threw a handful of broken coral over the fish and, with a flash of silver, the flying fish shot out of the swamp and soared away on their shimmering wings into the ocean.

Thanks to Kemiana's husband, there was good food to be caught in the sea and plenty for everyone to share.

AUSTRALIA
AND OCEANIA

SOURCES

The Ten Little Ostriches
The Masai: Their Language and Folklore by A. C. Hollis. Pub. The Clarendon Press 1905

Why the Cheetah's Cheeks Are Stained With Tears
When Hippo was Hairy by Nick Greaves. Pub. Struik 1988

Why Hippo Lives in Water
Folk Stories from Southern Nigeria by Elphinstone Dayrell. Pub. Longmans, Green & Co 1910

Ananse and the Python
Tales of an Ashanti Father by Peggy Appiah. Pub. Andre Deutsch 1967

The Ants and the Treasure
Yoruba Legends by M. I. Ogumefu. Pub. The Sheldon Press 1929

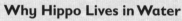

The Leopard and the Ram
West African Folk Tales collected by W. H. Barker and Cecilia Sinclair. Pub. C.M.S.

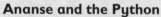

Why the Warthog is Ugly – Traditional

The Elephant and the Blind Men – Traditional

The White Butterfly
Myths and Legends of Japan by F. Hadland Davis. Pub. George G. Harrap & Co. 1912

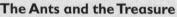

The Country of the Mice
Folk Tales of Tibet Collected and translated by Capt. W. F. OConnor. Pub. Hurst and Blackett Ltd 1907

The Farmer and the Mule – Traditional

The Lion and the Clever Jackals: *Old Deccan Days or Hindoo Fairy Legends* Collected by Mary Frere. Pub. John Murray 1898

Urashima and the Turtle
Green Willow and Other Japanese Fairy Tales by J. Grace. Pub. Macmillan & Co 1910

The Nodding Tiger
A Chinese Wonder Book by Norman Hinsdale Pitman. Pub. Dutton and Co. 1919

The Legend of the Panda – Traditional

How the Jellyfish Lost His Bones
Japanese Fairy Tales by Yei Theodora Ozaki. Pub. Grosset & Dunlap 1908

Buffalo and Eagle Wing – Traditional

Prairie Wolf
American Indian Fairy Tales by Margaret Compton. Pub. Dodd, Mead and Co. 1907

The Mermaid of the Magdalenes
Canadian Wonder Tales by Cyrus MacMillan. Pub. John Lane, The Bodley Head. 1920

Why the Swallow's Tail is Forked
The Book of Nature Myths by Florence Holbrook. Pub. Houghton, Mifflin & Co. 1902

Rabbit and the Moon Man
Canadian Wonder Tales by Cyrus MacMillan. Pub. John Lane, The Bodley Head. 1920

Why the Bear Has a Stumpy Tail
The Book of Nature Myths by Florence Holbrook. Pub. Houghton Mifflin & Co. 1902

The Blind Boy and the Loon
A Treasury of Eskimo Tales by Clara K. Bayliss. Pub. Thomas Y. Crowell & Co 1922

The First Woodpecker – Traditional

The Badger and the Bear *Old Indian Legends* by Zitkala-Sa. Pub. Ginn and Co. 1901

How the King of the Birds Was Chosen – Traditional

The Bear Prince – Traditional

Coyote and the Turtle
Fairy Tales of Mexico by Barbara Ker Wilson. Pub. Cassell & Dutton 1960

The Little Frog of the Stream
Latin American Tales by Genevieve Barlow. Pub. Rand, McNally & Co 1966

The Song of the Armadillo – Traditional

The Two Viscachas
The king of the Mountains by M.A. Jagendorf and R. S. Boggs. Pub. The Vanguard Press 1960

The Party in the Sky
Fairy Tales from Brazil by Elsie Spicer Eells. Pub. Dodd, Mead & Co. 1917

How the Beetles Got Their Gorgeous Coats
Fairy Tales from Brazil by Elsie Spicer Eells. Pub. Dodd, Mead & Co. 1917

The Nightingale
New Fairy Tales by Hans Christian Andersen. Pub. C.A. Reitzel 1843

The Three Billy Goats Gruff
East O the Sun, West O the Moon retold by Gudrun Thorne Thomsen. Pub. Row, Peterson & Co. 1912

The Owl of Cowlyd Coomb
Wild Wales by George Borrow. Pub. John Murray 1906

King of the Cats
Fairy Gold – A Book of Old English Fairy Tales chosen by Ernest Rhys. Pub. J. M. Dent & Co. 1913

Dapplegrim *The Red Fairy Book* by Andrew Lang. Pub. Longmans, Green and Co. 1890

The Eagle and the Wren
Scottish Fairy and Folk Tales. Selected by Sir George Douglas Bart. Pub. A. L. Burt and Co 1892

Saint Domnoc and the Bees
The Lives of the British Saints Vol. 2 by Baring-Gould and Fisher. Pub. The Honourable Society of Cymmrodorion 1908

The Three Little Pigs
The Green Fairy Book by Andrew Lang. Pub. Longmans, Green and Co. 1892

Mighty Mikko
Mighty Mikko Finnish Folk and Fairy Tales by Parker Fillmore. Pub. Harcourt, Brace & Co. 1922

The Speckled Hen – Traditional

The White Parrot
Tales of Enchantment from Spain Retold by Elsie Spicer Eells. Pub. Harcourt, Brace and Co. No date.

The Ugly Duckling
The Orange Fairy Book by Andrew Lang. Pub. Longmans, Green and Co. 1906

How the Kangaroo Got Her Pouch – Traditional

Nanaue, The Shark Boy *Hawaiian Folk Tales* Compiled by Thos. G. Thrum. Pub. A. C. McClurg & Co 1912

Paikea and Ruatapu
Te Ao Hou – The Māori Magazine No. 40 Pub. The Dept. of Māori Affairs 1962

Emu and the Brush Turkey
Folk Tales of the World – Australia by Rene Beckley. Pub. E. J. Arnold & Sons Ltd. 1965

How the Flying Fish Lived in a Tree
Papuan Fairy Tales by Annie Ker. Pub. Macmillan & Co 1910

Quarto is the authority on a wide range of topics.

Quarto educates, entertains and enriches the lives of our readers—enthusiasts and lovers of hands-on living.

www.quartoknows.com

First published in the UK in 2017 by Frances Lincoln Children's Books,
an imprint of The Quarto Group,
The Old Brewery, 6 Blundell Street, London N7 9BH QuartoKnows.com
Visit our blogs at QuartoKids.com

Important: there are age restrictions for most blogging and social media sites and in many countries parental consent is also required. Always ask permission from your parents. Website information is correct at time of going to press. However, the publishers cannot accept liability for any information or links found on any Internet sites, including third-party websites.

A catalogue record for this book is available from the British Library.

ISBN 978-1-78603-044-3

Illustrated in pencil and watercolour

Designed by Karissa Santos
Edited by Rebecca Fry
Published by Jenny Broom

Printed in China
1 3 5 7 9 8 6 4 2